A MIXTAPE OF WORDS

a fiction & nonfiction music anthology

A MIXTAPE OF WORDS

a fiction & nonfiction music anthology

LITTLE FICTION | BIG TRUTHS

2016 • littlefiction.com

Published by Inkshares Inc., San Francisco, California, as part of the Little Fiction | Big Truths Collection.

www.inkshares.com

Edited by Troy Palmer and Amanda Leduc.

Cover design by Troy Palmer.

Images from The Noun Project (thenounproject.com)

ISBN: 9781942645511

Library of Congress Control Number: 2016957185

First edition

Printed in the United States of America

A Mixtape Of Words

2016 LITTLE FICTION | BIG TRUTHS

Edited by Troy Palmer and Amanda Leduc. Cover design by Troy Palmer, with images from The Noun Project (thenounproject.com).

For more stories and essays visit littlefiction.com

THE PLAYLIST

INTRO

Foreword
by Troy Palmer | 9

SIDE A: NONFICTION

Elliott Smith Is Sad, Like You
by Sasha Chapin | 13

Mix Tape
by Wendy C. Ortiz | 27

God Is A DJ
by Mensah Demary | 49

Boiling Springs Rock City
by James Stafford | 63

Dance Outside Yourself
by Khanisha Foster | 75

Me & Iggy & John
by Troy Palmer | 87

Stop Reading and Listen
by Megan Stielstra | 103

SIDE B: FICTION

Analogue
by Jay Hosking | 125

I Don't Think So
by Christopher Evans | 149

My Lolita Experiment
by Leesa Cross-Smith | 155

If They Had Music
by Will Johnson | 161

Invisible Strings
by Steve Karas | 177

B-Sides
by Beth Gilstrap | 193

Thursday Night Karaoke
by Trevor Corkum | 209

HIDDEN TRACKS

The Songwriters | 219

Acknowledgements | 227

FOREWORD

by Troy Palmer

I'VE always been closer to music than I have been to books. Don't get me wrong, I love a good book (and a great story, of course) but music is always the first place I turn when I need to lose myself for a little while.

Growing up, music was how I defined myself. In high school, I was the weird (and for a short while, dreadlocked) kid who wore Butthole Surfers and Sub Pop World Domination Regime t-shirts and spent his most memorable nights going to see acts like Jane's Addiction, Doughboys, Public Enemy, and Wynton Marsalis (just to name a few).

Music is what I built friendships on. It was the yard stick I proudly judged others against and the tool I used for romance, on the odd occasion I needed a tool for romance. To this day, I probably still draw more inspiration from Chuck D than I do from Chuck Palahniuk. In fact, when I started Little Fiction | Big Truths (known then as just Little Fiction) I often drew parallels to music when discussing it—I wanted people to have a trust with Little Fiction the way I did (and still do) with record labels like Drag City, Sub Pop, and Stones Throw, and I saw our short story singles as mp3s of the writing world. Even then, I knew that I wanted to publish something to do with, or about, music. I just didn't know what that would look like until the idea for this anthology came along.

A Mixtape Of Words is a collection of fiction and nonfiction stories that explores every facet of how we interact with music and the many ways we turn to songs, albums, singers, songwriters, DJs, and musicians to help us get through love, death, divorce, and everything in between.

Put your headphones on. Turn it up.

Troy Palmer

Managing Editor, Little Fiction | Big Truths

NONFICTION

A

ELLIOTT SMITH IS SAD, LIKE YOU

by Sasha Chapin

ELLIOTT SMITH IS SAD, LIKE YOU

THE first time a girl ever called me pretty, she was absolutely stoned. Jessica from math class told me that my lips were beautiful, that my hair and my eyes were beautiful, and she handed me her headphones and asked me if I had ever heard the music of Elliott Smith. "He's amazing," she said. "He's sad, like you."

I was pretty sad back then. I spent a lot of time sitting in the corner of the school cafeteria, handling damp sandwiches and darkly wondering what a boob felt like. I played a baby in the school play, and when the unpopular girl playing my mother reached out to touch my spotlit face, someone shouted, unopposed, "Sasha's finally getting some action!" I wasn't actively planning to kill myself in the near future, but I sort of assumed I would, eventually. I was thankful that suicide was so vividly portrayed in movies and television.

I was pretty sad in 2003, but I wasn't sad like Elliott Smith. Smith was maybe the best melody writer since Schubert, but unlike Schubert, he was smoking crack to liven things up when his daily dose of heroin mellowed him out too much. That summer, Smith maintained a dizzying rotisserie of prescription drug habits, impressive even on the scale of a Los Angeles entertainer. He was still writing and recording beautifully, but in concert he was mentally disfigured. There's footage of his performances from this era, and I would strongly recommend you not watch it. In an attempt to get clean, he went to a quack Malibu detox doctor, who pumped him full of amino acids and sent him mewling into sobriety, where he encountered whatever the opiates were previously concealing. He stabbed himself a few weeks after I first heard his music, as I was staring down Jessica's lip-gloss.

Not knowing his biography, teenage me heard some of that suffering in his work. I heard someone who had lived a long time in a dark territory I was just starting to visit. I didn't like it. It scared me. I only became a fan years later, when I became truly, obnoxiously sad myself. I was working at a pizza restaurant and declaring my suicidal intentions during dinner service. "I think I'm gonna kill myself," I said to Naomi. "This margherita is going to table 42." I recently learned from William Todd Schultz's unfortunately named but fairly well-written biography, *Torment Saint,* that Elliott was fond of making similarly rash declarations. Before he left Portland for New York, he told his friends that they weren't responsible for what happened to him in Brooklyn—that they shouldn't blame themselves for what he had done. That's not a typo. He had started referring to himself in the past tense, as if he were haunting his own body.

• • •

There is probably no graceful way to say that I think Elliott Smith, famous musical suicide, may have been murdered. Yes, I'm afraid that I'm one of those people from the Internet. But, since the primary murder suspect in the case of Elliott Smith is Jennifer Chiba, his ex, I feel I should mention that I'm not one of these people who hates women for interfering in the lives of famous men—I have unconditional praise to offer Yoko Ono, and somewhat-conditional praise to offer Courtney Love. But there is a corner of his fanbase who are convinced that he didn't take his own life, and I have to confess that this idea gives me comfort.

It's tricky to diagnose suicidal intent even in the living. Someone can express suicidal urges without possessing the commitment to fulfill them. Elliott Smith professed suicidal urges on numerous occasions, but so did I. ("I know you're not really suicidal," my social worker friend said. "You're not fooling me.") I find it frustrating and not at all fulfilling to, as I have, Google accounts of Elliott's late life, attempting to comb them for clues.

Strangely, the thought exercise I find more compelling is to ask whether I would have killed myself if I were Elliott Smith—whether his life was one I or anyone would want to survive from the inside. By the way, have you heard the music of Elliott Smith? As Jessica told me in math class—he's amazing; he's sad, like you.

It might be tricky for me to expand on that. An artist you

love occupies a weird in-between place, where they're somehow a little more than a father, but a little less than a neighbour. They can permanently re-organize your consciousness but they can't sell you a Coke. You feel you know them more than anyone you actually know, which means that you don't really know a damn thing. I feel I know Elliott Smith, but if I picture him in front of me, I find myself picturing a tiny figurine, or Mount Rushmore. At five foot nine, he was slightly shorter than me, which feels incorrect.

Elliott Smith was born into a somewhat typical fucked up backstory—one slightly particular version of a kind of childhood that afflicts millions of people—which transformed into a highly atypical fucked up adult life, where he made a living by carefully enunciating the disgust his young life left him holding. For a living, he waded into the shit he was born into, and polished it into pearls. He had a sourceless displeasure that followed him everywhere, apparently unaffected by friendship, an Oscar nomination or anything else. Those close to him compared him to two widely celebrated archetypes of sadness: Eeyore and Kierkegaard. Someone you know is sort of like this—whether by genetics or Satan, they can't appreciate your love, or pizza. But that person you know probably isn't one of those monomaniacal artists, like Samuel Beckett, who got better at one thing than anybody else ever had. Smith's thing was being the McCartney of Methadone. He wrote melodies as irresistible as car commercial jingles about dreaming of a disappeared lover from a pool of drool in a dive bar. He liked to play with dissonance, threading these infectious melodies over arrangements filled with sighing blue notes and dizzy chords—the effect is that of a graceful ghost, traipsing effortlessly through a ruin. He sang with faint but perfect pitch about being a sloppy failure, over tight, elegant arrangements played by an enviable backup ensemble—Elliott Smith on drums, bass, and piano. Imagine Gaudi carving cathedrals stuck all over with renderings of a naked, puking Gaudi. That's about the scale of what we're dealing with here.

Joan Didion famously wrote, "We tell ourselves stories in order to live." I think she's right, but that it's frequently more to the point to say "we tell ourselves stories in order to stay inside watching Netflix and nursing our little sadness." You know how this feels. Whether through isolation or cocaine or compulsive spending, we engineer the circumstances we believe we deserve. Significant sadness is a constant companion, rich with wordy speculation, full of invitations to hundreds of quiet evenings spent clutching a sweat-stained mattress.

You know how it feels to deprive yourself. But Elliott was a virtuoso of this kind of privation, on a scale beyond (at least my) capability. He funded the substance habits that accelerated his misery with the music about that misery. He was fascinated by self-destruction. One of his best songs, "Needle in the Hay," is a paean to heroin he wrote five years before heroin ever touched his bloodstream. One of his girlfriends left him because, among other reasons, he couldn't shut up about wondering what it would like to be a heroin addict. Lou Reed once said: "You know, some people got no choice / and they can never find a voice to talk with that they can even call their own / So the first thing that they see / that allows them the right to be / why they follow it, you know, it's called bad luck."

I tend to hold with neurobiologist Robert Sapolsky in the

opinion that depression is the worst disease you can have. Cancer patients sometimes speak of the meaning that sudden mortality brings into their lives. The bizarre urge to continue being can drive people to even retrospectively enjoy the recovery from malaria, in that it provides a valley you can eye from subsequent happiness. The only thing that makes life worth living is your feeling that it is. Depression erodes that feeling with a powerful efficiency unmanageable even by bizarre, pervasive diseases of the skin. Elliott spent his life courting real depression, with great skill and fanatical devotion.

• • •

Some years before Elliott died, he jumped off a cliff. He didn't mean to kill himself then—not exactly. He started sobbing in a friend's car. When the friend tried to console him, Elliott leapt out of the car and bolted. It just so happened that the direction he chose took him to a precipice. He was drunk. He saw the edge coming, and thought, oh, I'm about to fall off a cliff, and the thought gave him no pause. Imagine this nightmare world: you wake up in the hospital with a nasty puncture wound after jumping, and as you lie there, itching your bandages, you think, I could turn this into a tight little couplet.

So you do—you write "Division Day," an irritatingly catchy jumper's anthem that Katy Perry could turn into a #1 hit, provided her team re-wrote all the words about being "naked except for a perpetual debt that couldn't be stripped away," or the ones about being "a grown man dying from fright," or the ones about "flying to fall away from you all." Listen to it twice, and you'll find yourself singing it in the shower, shampooing yourself to a depiction of approaching terminal velocity above a freezing ocean.

"Division Day" is a great microcosm of the problem of Elliott Smith's existence—the problem with having a way to make your suffering bearable is that you then have a way to make your suffering bearable. Former addicts of all kinds speak of the importance of bottoming out. You get to a place where your habit can no longer be seen as aesthetic—not a hobby, but a way of life. Maybe you're down to pawning stolen garden gnomes to get your Dilaudid. But in Smith's life, all suffering was instantly transformed by his prolific musical mind, remaining aesthetic by definition. Smith wrote, as far as I can tell, exactly two prevailingly happy songs. If being Elliott Smith sounds like a repetitious, stupid way to live, it might be helpful to know that Smith shared your disdain. He had a lot of insight into his condition. It just didn't help.

This insight reaches its peak in "King's Crossing," which is, I feel, Smith's best work. It's also his most horrifying. The intro is so pretty that when I listen to it I can't feel my legs. From sinister mumbling comes a cloud of inbent melody which clears abruptly over retro electric ragtime piano, playing a figure equally nostalgic and martian. Do you ever come to a moment of awareness where you look coolly around yourself and go, "I guess this is my fucking life?" Elliott Smith, in "King's Crossing," auditions himself for the role of himself—"read the part and return at five," he sings, "it's a hell of a role if you can keep it alive." He realizes that he's a caricature of his own worst tendencies, played out for the benefit of his handlers, that "the method acting that pays [his] bills keep the fat man feeding in Beverly Hills." He knows the part very well, to the point that he can clearly see its logical final act—"I've seen the movie," he sings, "and I know what happens." What happens is his dealer arrives (his dealer is, hilariously, compared to Santa Claus) bearing heroin that lands Smith in a hospital where "time reverses and dead men talk to all the pretty nurses"—he is talking about himself, once again, posthumously. Amidst all this, he sings "gimme one good reason not to do it," over a chorus of his own overdubbed falsetto pronouncing a long, evolving, wordless vowel. Go ahead—he's asking you a question.

• • •

When I'm thinking about Elliott Smith, sometimes I'm also thinking about how suicidal doesn't necessarily mean suicide. I hope you can't relate to me at all when I say that suicidal can be a place where you can live for a long time. Not the act of suicide, of course, but suicide as a framework for living. Apologies for the Nietzsche quotation: "The thought of suicide is a great consolation: by means of it one gets through many a dark night." It's so fucking true, though. You can endure a lot of torment by silently imagining how everyone you know will react to the news of your hanging. You can privately curate a list of bridges, balconies, and likely last words. Despite everything you're helpless to change—acne, poverty, your central perversion, whatever—with suicide your control is, in the most literal sense, final.

Elliott Smith actually would rarely sing about committing

suicide. Most often he sung about being cynical—about the disappointing future sprawling before him. His most romantic song, "Say Yes," is about feeling philosophical and grown up about losing the love of your life. The central difference between a cynic and a suicide, I think, is that the cynic believes that life is definitely worth barely living. A real cynic is ravenous for more romantic frustration, more stupors, more cigarettes. Cynicism offers an inverted version of the comfort of religion—it saturates everything with shitty meaning.

In "Waltz 2," Smith sang, "I'm never gonna know you now, but I'm gonna love you anyhow." The line is specifically about his mother, but it feels more general. It feels like the song of someone who more easily loves people he doesn't know—who can only truly adore people whose love he hasn't had the chance to sabotage. It feels like the lament of someone in an exclusive relationship with their prideful despair—someone who watches drunks stumbling from a packed club, thinking, "I wish I could be one of those morons." I know people like that. I used to be one of them. I maybe still kind of am. We don't die—we'd hate to confirm our suspicions of your suspicions of our weakness—we live to prove you wrong. Elliott always maintained that he loved making his music, even as his music usually claimed that he didn't love much at all.

One of Elliott's last songs, "Suicide Machine," is about being really annoyed that people think you want to kill yourself. The song's lead vocals were recorded the day before his death. A lot of people thought Elliott might not make it. That makes murdering Elliott Smith the perfect crime. The day that he died, blood was smeared all over Elliott's house. Responding to allegations that Elliott's death was suspicious, Jennifer Chiba told the press that she and Elliott's family knew the truth—that he definitely killed himself. His blood relatives summarily issued a press release clarifying that she was not, in fact, speaking on behalf of the Smith family. She subsequently sued them for a portion of the estate. Having taken first aid, I know that you shouldn't pull a sharp object out of a wound. Jennifer Chiba, having taken first aid, certainly knows that too, and yet she pulled Elliott's knife from Elliott's wound.

I know this is all totally crazy. But I can't help it. Elliott Smith's death is a permanent moment of discomfort in my imagination, like a tattoo that healed a little blotchy. The human mind is terrible at tolerating ambiguity. I find it very difficult to live in a world where Elliott Smith *maybe* killed himself, though I know that's the only reasonable option.

The secondary tragedy of a completed suicide is how it can make someone's whole life seem like a suicide in progress. An acquaintance of mine committed suicide a few years after we played basketball one summer. Absurd things have happened to my memories of that game—I've tried to search my recollections of his dribbling for symptoms of lovelessness. I can't help but feel there was some melancholy behind his gorgeous smile that day, even knowing, as I do, that in all likeliness all his smile concealed was the neural substrate of basketball. Similarly, I find myself engaged in wild, astrological supposing whenever I listen to Elliott's music—wondering whether one can hear suicide in the swooning upper voice of a harmony.

• • •

There's no real beginning or end to this story I'm telling you, but I went looking for one at the house where Elliott Smith died, in Echo Park. I wasn't in Los Angeles to pay my respects—I was there because I had one of those impossible love affairs that bring you up against the walls of your life only to discover that they're as durable as dead leaf. The relationship started in Toronto, then attained a silly level of sincerity over Skype. We agreed that I had to fly out to California to see if the love we had was real. It wasn't, quite. We agreed as much one evening over a bottle of pinot noir that tasted like mouldy lipstick. We didn't really want to look at each other so I went walking to the CVS to grab some toilet paper. It was raining approximately seventeen drops of rain—the piteous rain of a prolonged drought—and I was in a bleak mood, the kind of mood where you Google "elliott smith death house echo park address suicide murder," and discover that you're right in front of the house where Elliott Smith died. It was on the way to the toilet paper, maybe three hundred meters from where I was staying.

Elliott Smith's house is a box. It's a box on Lemoyne Street, a lovely diagonal stroll between mature oak and olive trees, punctuated by guard dogs saying hello from behind fences hiding the human sources of clouds of high-grade THC. You can walk down a secret staircase past a tiny fruit orchard, down to the corner of Echo and Sunset, where there are dollar tacos and three dollar hot dogs with onion salad, cooked with bacon fat in divoted skillets. You can get mugged, as I did, by skilled American muggers, who will disabuse you of your funds quickly and painlessly.

Elliott Smith's house is not a box that bespeaks musical mastery. It's not particularly suggestive of darkness or misery. Certainly there are no bloodstains. You don't even feel a well-defined lack, as with a hollow being prepared for a skyscraper's foundation. You may see, as I did, the silhouette of a person gazing back at you from the window, a person used to people gawking with ill-defined facial expressions at the box where Elliott Smith died.

You hear people talking about closure, or letting go. "Letting go is the only sane way to live," a Buddhist once monk told me, shortly before claiming he could cure diabetes with a massage. I appreciate the sentiment, but I think the language is weak. "Closure" offers the metaphor of the past as a music-box with a delicate, delicately closing clasp. "Letting go" implies that the past is a kite I'm hesitating to give to the air it prefers. Maybe it's like that for you. For me, though, adult life is full of an unknowing that is not at all like a charm or a kite. Something very bad happens in Syria that you don't even notionally understand. Your friends disappear to other cities, or to consuming careers, or they just disappear—it's impressive, how easily and totally people can vanish. There's this fog of unknowing that surrounds you, and, sometimes, you see a face staring back at you from inside. Elliott Smith was in a dream I had last week. He was off to the side of a distended greenhouse, half-obscured by a stand of tall white grass, looking like he was searching for something.

Increasingly I find myself turning to the past and saying, I love you, but I wish you would just shut up.

MIX TAPE

by Wendy C. Ortiz

1."LOSING MY RELIGION" BY R.E.M

The song title reminded me of religion classes I was forced to attend in Catholic school.

Operation Desert Storm was a month old. I was a senior in high school attending protests against the war. I had literally lost my religion several years before. I used to read the Bible, to silently call to God for wishes, for rescue, until just before I met the junior high teacher who would become my lover.

At seventeen, when the song came out, my teacher was less in my life than before. He had already told me, after mountains of Sunday brunch buffet food and a load of mimosas and mini-champagne bottles, that he loved me, had always been in love with me, as we sat at that hilltop restaurant in Burbank that later burned down.

In one of our conversations, growing fewer as I neared the legal age of eighteen, he told me "Losing My Religion" was one of his favorite songs. Because, he said, he could relate. I remembered his early Catholicism, which seemed like a costume he'd worn as a child, discarding when he hit college.

He was one of the most reckless, drug-addled, sexually perverse adults I knew.

I ran with this image, this idea of 'losing one's religion.' Did Jeff understand that this was a Southern expression, a way of describing righteous anger, the act of losing one's temper? I certainly didn't.

The song, which still plays on the radio oracle in my car at least once a week on various radio stations, has a tendency to make me think of the first time Jeff and I had sex, if you could call it that, on my mother's living room couch.

After he left that day, he called me from a pay phone, anxious, breathing hard, dare I say hysterical. *I just broke the* cardinal *rule of teaching,* he cried.

I was fourteen and couldn't give a flying fuck. I wanted our affair to continue so I tried to talk him down. I never forgot those words because the word *cardinal* was something I associated with Catholicism. I'd already stopped reading the bible, stopped praying to God, shifted from the heavy rotation of Depeche Mode and skipped backward to the music of Jeff's youth in some effort to connect. In fact, I behaved as though this man was my religion. Weed and Ecstasy and LSD were the eucharists of this new religion.

Oh no I've said too much

Years later we were on that hillside overlooking the Valley I'd grown up in, at the restaurant that would burn down after I moved a thousand miles away. At that moment, I, seventeen; he, thirty-two, whatever religions we'd clung to, shapeshifted into something we couldn't quite recognize anymore.

I haven't said enough

2. "LIFE DURING WARTIME" BY TALKING HEADS "TAKE ME TO THE RIVER" BY AL GREEN, PERFORMED BY TALKING HEADS

Heard of a van that's loaded with weapons

Packed up and ready to go

On one of the bong-smoke-filled afternoons at that house in Van Nuys, Jeff explained to me the lyrics of the song "Life During Wartime." It was music he'd listened to when he was in college.

Listen, he said. *This is a song about the IRA. The Irish Republican Army. Young people who are used to war and have given their lives over to what's important rather than some bullshit fun and games.*

I pretended like I knew what he was talking about. *Irish, huh?* I knew Jeff was Irish, but what army and what war was he speaking of? I didn't ask.

I liked Talking Heads, but knew more of their 1980s songs than their 1970s songs. I had written a short story in seventh grade based on the song "Road to Nowhere," when I still wrote stories that wound their way through looping mystery and horror territory, ending in destruction.

I luxuriated instead in the silk fog wrapped around my head, the remains of his semen dripping down my thigh that I hadn't wiped off, and his voice, his direct conversation with me, his attention. Sixteen, I thought I was in love with the man explaining lyrics to me.

The song is not actually about the IRA. It's about New York.

Jeff told me once, later, while he was living in an apartment alone—a rarity—that he met a homeless guy and started talking to him and eventually invited him to come and sleep at his place because, *fuck! it's the least I could do! And it's nothing, really!*

In a way this was shocking to me, and also unsurprising. Jeff was one of the first adults in my life to point to social injustice.

At the tender age of thirteen, when we met, I was particularly sensitive to injustice. I felt it when I entered the mall in my all-black outfit with heavily eyelinered eyes and bangs hair-sprayed straight up. I felt it when my parents kept me at home with the fumes of their alcohol-soaked weekends threatening to suffocate me. I felt a low-grade chronic thrum of injustice whenever I was with Jeff. When he refused to kiss me. When he called the shots of almost every facet of our relationship.

Later, when I got to college, I began my love affair with Talking Heads in earnest. I listened to "Life During Wartime" and kept wondering why CBGB was in the song. That was a club in New York, right? So why was it in this song?

In those years, my early twenties, I believed my calling was to confront every social justice I could see or uncover.

A member of Sinn Féin, the left-wing Irish political party, came to my little college hidden in the forest of the Pacific Northwest, and I went to hear the speaker, partly because I was a political economy student and felt the pressure of going, partly because my secret crush Seanna was going, and partly because in some weird way, it might make me feel closer to the man I had already left behind, but who would haunt me for years, in the ways one is haunted by Someone Who Fucked You Up.

I don't know why I love you like I do

All the changes you put me through

Years earlier, I'd written these words, in block capital letters, on sheets of paper that I snuck to Mr. Ivers, before I deigned to call him Jeff (that mysteriously spelled, one-syllable, bite of a name). It was my way of telling him: *you're fucking me up. I love how you're fucking me up. But you're fucking me up.*

I'll never know what happened to the various missives I had the courage to write him over the years, the letters always heavy with various lyrics. I imagine the smoke curling up into thin black wisps, his lighter flicking on and off, the papers folding into themselves, disintegrating into ash.

3. "TAKE A CHANCE ON ME" BY ABBA "DOES YOUR MOTHER KNOW" BY ABBA

Because lyrics told the stories I couldn't yet tell. Because lyrics could be code, could be short-hand to telling someone how deep I wanted to go with them. And because I was slightly aware that

ABBA might not be cool at all, because it was music I listened to with my parents when I was a little girl, I wrote out the lyrics and cited it ARTIST UNKNOWN in purple ink.

If you change your mind I'm the first in line

With all of my thirteen year old heart, I wanted my teacher to know that I could be whatever he wanted me to be, and he didn't have to wait until I was eighteen for my sake. When he broke up with his girlfriend over and over, a broken record of misery that made him drunk and compelled him to keep his phone off the hook, a symbol of his disconnect to everything, I wanted him to know I was still willing, and that though I'd never had a boyfriend, I could be the girlfriend he always dreamed of.

Whatever that was.

He brought a photo of his girlfriend to school once. We'd already been talking on the phone for a few weeks. He'd already told me he wanted to go down on me. He'd already asked me to come to school with a short skirt and no leggings, which I never did.

The photo was of a buxom, dark curly-haired woman in a bikini with supple, olive skin.

I wore glasses, had short hair, covered up as much skin as I could, wore gothy make-up and boots and a constant blank look on my face that I worked hard to maintain.

She was clearly a *woman*. A woman with a mysterious sexy name, someone who *had* him. Had him salivating and gushing and red and showing off her photo to his eighth grade English students.

She was my competition. Okay.

I listened, biting my lip, as he told me about her breaking up with him. Of her cross-country, job-related move. Of their daily phone calls, and how he could tell her what kind of underwear she was wearing from 3000 miles away, because he knew her that well.

I got drunk on wine coolers in my bedroom on the nights I knew they were out on a date.

I secretly celebrated whenever they broke up, with wine coolers in my bedroom.

I would meet her a few years later. It was one of those Saturdays I happened by his house.

Who knows when I'd fucked him last but we'd been fucking off and on for some time. I was stopping by before I went to my boyfriend's band practice where I'd have to sit around for hours getting drunk on Boone's Farm before I might leave and have sloppy sex with my drunk-off-his-ass boyfriend.

Jeff's garage door was open. I parked, not having seen her yet. I'd thought for a moment that I was sure to get a joint and a *let me show you around my garage* and maybe get a nooner kind of visit.

His girlfriend popped out from behind something and I kept the composure everyone was starting to know me for. Neck regal. Feet in rainbow Converse tennis shoes firmly planted (I was a hippie, now), standing across from an A-line skirt, arm-baring sweater, short heels.

She was kind, she was courteous, and she said, *Jeff has told me so much about you.* I thought of when he told me how she'd asked who I was after seeing a photo of me on his mantle. *One of the smartest students I have*, he'd told me, *who's gonna go on to be brilliant at whatever she does.*

I did the intelligent thing and accepted the social niceties and made up a reason why I had just dropped by and then I got out of there. Huffing as I unwrapped a fresh pack of cigarettes and pretended I wasn't crying and fuming all at once, trudging away from a scene I couldn't really explain to anyone at the time.

Oh you can take your time baby, I'm in no hurry, know I'm gonna get you

His girlfriend left him for good not long after. She was always leaving him.

I was always arriving, on foot, by bus, by stepping out of the cars of strangers.

Ah, but girl you're only a child

4. "BRING ON THE DANCING HORSES" BY ECHO AND THE BUNNYMEN

We met when I wore a uniform of black clothing and heavy make-up that I applied after my father dropped me off at school or the public bus stop. We met when I was reconsidering bible study. We met when I was writing letters to a guy in prison who I'd found in the back of the *LA Weekly* advertising for pen pals and when I was writing letters to my former English teacher who'd returned to Boston with his fiancée. We met when I was still praying that my parents would stop drinking. We met when my parents were reaching their ultimate hate crescendos. We met when I contemplated just how I might run away, just how I might kill myself and make those parents sorry. We met when I was just starting to understand that men in the world found me alluring for some inexplicable reason, and I thought the reason was for my darkness, and in fact, I was partly right. The silences I could keep. The hardened stare with pout lips. The coolness and the supposed depth they might try to swim in me.

Shiver and say the words of every lie you've heard

I was really a thirteen year old who would rather read books than do anything else, because life inside my head was much better than life in front of my eyes. I was really a girl who was learning about power and its underbelly, getting in cars with strangers, monitoring the slow flow of adrenaline as it pumped through me each time I pulled a door closed, smelled the scent of an unfamiliar car, plotting a way to get where I needed to go, sometimes having to do things I'd rather not do, sometimes having to do nothing but give directions to my destination. I was really an adolescent who put a lot of stock in songs and poetry that I started writing in red and blue marker on the walls of my bedroom, inhaling the toxic smells, burning incense to cover up the pot smoke, feeling every single hair on my head scream when I listened to my music loud with marijuana urging me along. I was writing on the walls to my mother's dismay. But she couldn't stop me.

First I'm gonna make it then I'm gonna break it til it falls apart

This was a romantic refrain to me, something I carried

with me through my twenties, allowing it to edge in, slither around my head, around the glass that my fingers were holding that transported amber liquids into my body, my belief that I was a destroyer. An astrologer had told me so, after all.

See the way Mars and Pluto are situated in your chart? You are here to destroy.

Well, then, I said. *Let us begin.*

5. "BUS STOP" BY THE HOLLIES

From day one, in his classroom and outside of his classroom, Jeff crooned old music, often changing the lyrics to suit him. Fifteen, before I had my learner's permit or access to my mother's car, I stitched together my passage from home to all the areas of the Valley I wanted to lose myself in.

Bus stop Wendy she's here asking

Please share my umbrella

Jeff and his friend and sometime housemate Ed sat at their dining room table talking. I pulled out a seat and sat down with a sigh after a few moments of standing awkwardly in the living room, wishing for an invitation. I slipped off my sandals and let my feet touch the carpet.

So, Jeff began, looking at the glass tabletop, *how's Bus Stop Wendy?*

Fine, I said, looking from his face to Ed's. Ed smiled broadly at me. We met one of the numerous Saturdays I happened by, records in hand, wishes blooming in my chest.

But I didn't ride the bus here, I said, picking up my bag and looking inside for a lighter or some matches. *I hitched.*

I felt Jeff looking at me. He sighed sharply, stood up. Ed watched him and then looked at me and shrugged. I knew Ed was attracted to me. He made it obvious. I looked away, itchy and nervous.

I'm going to explain this once, and once only, Jeff said before he left the room.

He came back with two pairs of knee-high stockings. My lip curled when I saw them. I was reminded of my mother's wardrobe, the drawer that held such strange items as knee-highs and pantyhose, tan, limp pieces of fine mesh.

Why do you have those? I finally laughed, finding my voice.

Yeah, man, what are you doing *with those ugly things?* Ed asked.

Wendy, sit back in that chair, Jeff replied.

I looked up at him and laughed. I settled deeper into the chair and he used a hand to push my chest back, straight, my back flush with the chair back.

So. Let's say you're out there in the world, and you're hitchhiking. Jeff was talking to me in a sing-song voice I immediately didn't like. He lengthened one knee-high stocking in his hands and threw the other three on the table.

And some guy picks you up and you tell him where you wanna go, but he takes you somewhere else. Someplace you haven't been, and don't want to be. Jeff began tying one of my ankles to the chair leg with the hosiery. *Too tight?* he asked, looking up at me.

A little, I answered, my eyes wide, trying to form a casual smile that wouldn't come.

Good. He took another stocking off the table and tied my other ankle to the chair. *If it were someone else, they might use a cord. Or electrical tape. Or rope.*

What the fuck, Jeff, I finally stammered as he bent one of my arms back and tied it behind me to the metal arm of the chair. I could not look at Ed; this suddenly felt private and insane, a flaw in Jeff's composition, something I had always wondered about, but could never put my finger on.

When both of my arms and legs are tied to the chair I said again, weakly, *What the fuck.*

Oh, wait, one more thing. Jeff stomped to his bedroom and returned with a bandanna.

I get it, already, I began, resting my eyes on Ed.

Jeff, man, she gets the picture, Ed said, taking his eyes off my tied ankles for a moment. Jeff raised one finger at him and turned back to me.

Okay, Wendy. You hitchhike, and this is but one possible fate. Do you know there are people out there who will do this to you and any other girl that's out on the street looking to get from one place to another? I mean, how can I make you understand? Look, I have a fucking hard-on here, he said, smacking his crotch through his pants with an open palm. I looked down at the smoke-scented bandanna on my mouth and felt sleepy. My nostrils flared like they do right before I start crying.

You don't want to get raped. You don't want someone to do this to you. But when you get into their car, you don't know who you're fuckin' dealing with. Some asshole, maybe? You'll never know. He paused dramatically. He untied the bandanna from around my mouth.

Tell me, Ed, did it not turn you on to see a pretty young thing tied up like that? Jeff said, turning to Ed matter-of-factly as I shook my arms and legs out, the stockings falling to the carpet like small, shed skins.

Oh, Jeff, man, she understood, she understood, Ed said. *Why are you friends with this guy?* Ed said, turning to me.

My tongue ran over my lips.

Can I have some water? I asked, already hating the demure tone I hear in my voice.

Jeff moved into the kitchen, retrieved a mug. He let the tap run, filling the mug. He handed it to me with both hands, touching mine as I received it. I drank. My heart slowed, beat faintly.

Don't hitchhike to get here, okay? That's all I ask, he said when I put the mug down. He gave me a playful kick under the table. I kicked back, stung, speechless.

Let's have a smoke, shall we?

I licked my lips again, wishing for more water. Soon a joint was being born on the glass tabletop.

6. "FORTRESS AROUND YOUR HEART" BY STING

Under the ruins of a walled city

Months after my eighteenth birthday, I visited Jeff in yet

another residence, this one across the Valley, this time shared with one of his many cousins. When I pulled up to the house, located in a well-to-do suburbia I rarely frequented, I immediately felt like a visitor to another planet.

His cousin answered the door, a nerdy balding guy who politely let me in and then disappeared somewhere inside the house. Jeff received me and his booming voice reminded me that we were still in hiding and his cousin might be listening.

As I return across the fields I'd known

He ushered me into his bedroom, and without giving me time to look around and notice this new place where I would not be visiting again, he presented me with a gift.

I recognized the fields where I'd once played

I opened up a card that was margin to margin full of his small, shaky handwriting. I couldn't take in everything written there, so pushed ahead to unwrap the gift.

It was a Tiffany stained glass, an image of a river flowing to the ocean under a bright sun. Jeff rambled something about the meaning of it, how we were rivers that would meet the sea? Or I was the river and he was the sea? I felt the presence of his strange cousin in the house and wanted to hurry the visit along. I wouldn't read the card closely until I got home, after stashing the stained glass back in its box, not knowing what to do with it.

Underneath the congratulations on graduating from high school, the wishes for a happy eighteenth birthday, were the complete lyrics to a song by Sting. A song that had come out the year before we met, when I was twelve. At eighteen I felt like I was psychologically light years from Sting, what he represented at the time. I was frequenting punk shows and Dead shows and Sting, was like, an old man.

My feelings for Sting were not too different from what I was feeling for Jeff.

Had to stop in my tracks for fear

Of walking on the mines I'd laid

I knew we were looking for an ending.

7. THE BLUES (public radio stations and the Long Beach Blues Festival)

It was cool and relaxed on the lawns. Everyone was friendly and smiling and Jeff shared a joint he brought with me and a man and woman nearby. They were sitting on a pastel-colored blanket and sipping at wine coolers bought from the concession stands. Jeff nodded at one and said, *Want me to go get you one?*

I nodded and my eyes followed him as he bent a knee against the grass, pushed himself up with a grunt and stood over me. *Don't run away now*, he joked, and pushed his glasses up on his nose.

I knew he noticed every man who turned in my direction, and his response was to lean closer to me or look me in the eye and shake his head like he couldn't believe their rudeness.

With Jeff gone, my eyes devoured the crowd, the bobbing heads, the walking forms of people safe in their adulthood. I swallowed and willed myself to take deep breaths, aware that I was young here, alone, just turned eighteen, and that it would be awhile before Jeff got back to this patch of grass.

I was alone in a sea of people who loved the blues. Everyone waited for the genius of B.B. King to take the stage. This was the umpteenth concert of my young life, and light years different from what I was used to at concerts. Everyone had a stony semblance of calm and happiness, a contentment that felt like milk over hot skin, soothing and exciting at once. I turned and looked, thinking I heard Jeff's voice, but he was nowhere in sight. My eyes returned to the stage and I tapped a bare foot against the grass, the sun falling down the length of the sky.

Before I made it to my boyfriend's house that evening, I endured countless pinpricks of innuendo that Jeff pressed into, against me. In the car, navigating the parking lot traffic on our way home, his mouth slightly open, I thought of his teeth. I knew the feel of my tongue in the gap between the top two. A sense of random endearment flooded me, a bizarre and new feeling of wanting to protect him.

It would be just a few months later when we attempted a leaving off with one another, the sound of nighttime tide accompanying the separation, and months after that, the painful crush of kisses in a parked car that would make our ending final.

8. "LOVE IS THE DRUG" BY ROXY MUSIC

Ain't no big thing

To wait for the bell to ring

Here's what I did.

I swallowed sleeping pills. I ate laxatives. My body melted down and thickened up, up and down, equivalent to the lust and denial I was living off of.

Jump up bubble up what's in store

I went on a date with one of Jeff's friends. Became intimate with other of his friends. I slept with a number of men the whole time I was "with" Jeff, under his influence—attempts to fuck his memory and his inattention and his meaningless words out of my body. My boyfriend knew and broke up with me. Then we got back together and I resumed my sluthood.

Love is the drug and I need to score

I met a man I liked and when it was clear he was into me, I lied about my age. It wasn't a big age difference—I was 19, he was 27, but he had to learn that I was not 20, but *turning* 20 after we'd been together for a while. It was the first lie I told him.

Stitched up tight can't break free

After escaping to the forest a thousand miles north of my home, ensconced in college, I met another man who came in the form of my apartment manager who reminded me strongly of Jeff. This man was married, clinically depressed, had a room full of martial arts weapons and liked taking runs around the lake by our apartment building. It was on one of these runs that I told him about Jeff.

Love is the drug got a hook in me

It seemed inexplicable at the time.

Soon, this man was asking me out for coffee. Soon, this

man was professing his attraction to me. In this instance, I did something different.

I started seeing a woman who I would talk to weekly in an office downtown. I started telling the story of me and Jeff to someone who could remind me what it all really might mean, and what it absolutely did not mean. From her couch I'd watch pigeons walking around the nearby rooftop. I spent ten years in this woman's presence, unraveling story lines, piecing others together, braiding some, taking scissors to others.

I stopped getting high but I got drunk a lot.

I looked back at my junior high and high school diaries.

I started writing the story of us.

Dancing at the only club in my newly adopted town in the Pacific Northwest, "Love is the Drug" playing, I felt the kind of blushing fuck-me-ness you can't really explain to anyone and don't want to explain because you just want to feel it and move with it and remember, maybe, where it began, even in its darkest, most unholy beginnings.

Oh oh catch that buzz

The song still has the power to make me want to pull over, walk into a bar and hear the ice clink around some liquid that will start a raging fire in me.

As I entered my thirties, I considered that I was now in the age range where Jeff had been when we parted. I got married at the age he was when we broke things off. I got divorced the year after. I fell in love with a woman who has many qualities that remind me of Jeff—her humor, her charisma, the way she confessed the hold I had on her, the manner in which she'd tell me she wanted to fuck me. All of it reminiscent of him.

It's complicated.

Love is the drug I'm thinking of

We made our own mixed CDs for each other during our courtship. Our seven month age difference means we grew up with much of the same music. A different vocabulary of melodies and riffs and lyrics took up space in my brain. We can make each other laugh with all the song lyrics we know that no one else knows we know. We sing songs to each other at The Smogcutter, a karaoke dive bar on Normal Street in Hollywood.

At dinner with friends one night in downtown Los Angeles I heard the overwhelm of Arcade Fire above the din.

I excused myself, stood, made my way around the maze of chairs and tables and people toward the bathroom.

I carry the names of the songs and the artists of my favorite mix tapes. I hold the order of them inside my body, where they are left intact, never to be cut, melted by heat, unspooled.

In the square of the private bathroom the speakers belted out the music I would come to think of as soundtrack to the life I had a hand in authoring, more so than previous lives I've lived.

The music pounded into me. I gripped the sink. I closed my eyes.

I took it in.

GOD IS A DJ

by Mensah Demary

1. James Yancey died on February 10, 2006, three days after his birthday. He was thirty-two.

2. *Donuts* was Mr. Yancey's ninth studio album, released on February 7, 2006. In its basic form, the album is a beat CD, a collection of instrumentals produced by Mr. Yancey. The album consists of thirty-one tracks.

3. There is only one track that is over two minutes in length—"Don't Cry"—and the album, in whole, clocks in at a little over forty-three minutes.

4. There are no emcees on *Donuts*. There are no hooks. No background vocalists. But there are lyrics.

5. *In 2002,* [Mr. Yancey] *was diagnosed with a rare blood disorder known as thrombotic thrombocytopenic purpura (TTP), which decreased his platelet count drastically and restricted blood flow to his kidneys and heart, leaving him weak. But weakness was unfamiliar territory to* [Mr. Yancey]. *He had never been weak-spirited, he didn't make weak beats, he didn't kick weak raps and he damn sure wasn't going to let his illness prevent him from doing what he loved. [1]*

6. The sublime beauty of *Donuts* lies in its depths, its corners, where a dead man left behind messages.

7. What would you create—you, the so-called artist—if you knew you had days left to live? The gods, they do not smile at Internet essays. They shrug their shoulders at website analytics and impressions. What will you tell them—so-called artist—when the gods ask you about your art? Will you tell them about the years spent creating content? Will you say you failed to make art because you never work for exposure?

8. *The record company issued a brief note about the title: Easy explanation.* [Mr. Yancey] *likes donuts. Yesterday his mother managed a chuckle when she confirmed that fact. I just bought two dozen a week ago, she said. [2]*

9. I purchased *Donuts* from iTunes sometime in February 2006. I lived in Georgia. My first depressive episode loomed, as did my first divorce. By February 2007, I would be in New Jersey.

10. My immediate reaction to *Donuts* was bewilderment. Mr. Yancey did create, on the surface, a beat CD. But no emcee would be foolish enough to rap over these beats. The drums were muted—almost irrelevant—while the samples' volumes were increased. I was confused. The samples were too loud to rap over, although emcees have since tried, to varying degrees of failure.

11. *Like his idol, Pete Rock, he let his music speak for him. [3]*

12. The jig was up, as they say, the first time I heard track number six, "Stop." Drums barely present—pitter-patting in the background, like a kitten rapping its paws on a snare—the beat

opens with a sample of emcee Jadakiss and his signature high-pitched *A-HA!* laugh, as though Mr. Yancey wanted our undivided attention. Demanded it. And so, in saunters Dionne Warwick as she sings, "You're gonna want me back / in your arms / You're gonna need me / one day / You're gonna want me back / in your arms." The sample is looped further, as Dionne sings "You better stop, and think about what you doing / You better stop, and think about what you're doing / You better stop..."

13. [Here, Mr. Yancey stops the track entirely, causing a one-second moment of silence]

14. "...and think about what you're doing."

15. Who was Mr. Yancey talking to? I asked myself as "Stop" abruptly ends, and the next donut begins.

16. The album, by now on its sixteenth track, is more than half over. Mr Yancey will be dead by the end.

17. On August 29, 2006, The Roots released *Game Theory*, their

seventh studio album. It is bookended by beats produced by Mr. Yancey. The album's final track, "Can't Stop This," features the donut "Time: The Donut of the Heart." This is meant to be a tribute to Mr. Yancey, but Black Thought—emcee for The Roots and one of the greatest battle rappers to ever walk the earth—sounds uncomfortable over the beat. Its melody is a sped-up sample of "All I Do Is Think of You" by The Jackson 5, but the sample's volume remains high. Black Thought rapped over Mr. Yancey's message; the end result is jarring, and not terribly enjoyable.

18. The other two samples on "Time: The Donut of the Heart" are

  18.1 "Yes It's You"

  18.2. and "Strangers in the Night."

19. "Airworks" is one of my favorite donuts, and I like to think I understand the message. When I listen to *Donuts*, I often imagine Mr. Yancey in the final weeks of his life, health in shambles, short of breath, terror in his wide eyes. "Airworks" contains one sample, "I Don't Really Care" by L.V. Johnson. Mr. Yancey sped up the sample, and chopped the vocals, taking what has already existed and transforming it into something new. The result is—at least how it sounds to me—the sample asking for air. Or letting the listener know that air is in short supply. "Oh no air," one part of the sample says—I believe.

20. *During an extended hospital stay last summer,* [Mr. Yancey's] *friends from the L.A.-based indie label Stones Throw came to his aid. "They brought him a little Boss [SP] 303 sampler and little 45 record player," says his close friend and fellow producer Karriem Riggins. "That's what brought him through to make a lot of music that we hear on Donuts." [4]*

21. The sample listing for another favorite of mine, "One Eleven":

21.1 "A Legend in its Own Time

21.2 "Here We Go"

22. I've known for almost nine years now that one day, I would do this: write my own *Donuts* and compile it into an essay, if this could be considered an essay. I will spare you the threadbare etymology of *essay*. This is an essay because I say it is, the way *Donuts* is a masterpiece, the way Mr. Yancey set out to create a masterpiece. This is *genius* I'm speaking about, the undeterred forward motion toward a finished product. *Donuts* is a piece of art, the seminal work of man who I've outlived, so far, by two years. Mr. Yancey would've never finished *Donuts* without the threat of impending death. Mr. Yancey would've finished *Donuts* had he lived on in good health, and the beats would sound similar—if one were to take a beat from the *Donuts* of this reality, and compared it with a beat from the *Donuts* in an alternate reality where Mr. Yancey still lives—but they would never be the same.

23. "Gobstopper" is the best donut.

24. Mr. Yancey produced two donuts with one record, "To The Other Man."

25. *In fact,* [Mr. Yancey] *completed 29 of the 31 songs on the aforementioned Donuts instrumental LP, his latest masterful release, while still in the hospital. The album was released through Stones Throw on* [Mr. Yancey's] *32nd birthday—only three days before he passed away. [5]*

26. We're all going to die.

27. "U-Love," the twenty-seventh track, contains a simple message, "Just because I really love you / Just because I really love you… love you… love you, you… I love you, you…" and on it goes for sixty one seconds. Mr. Yancey, short on time, opted for brevity.

28. Next, "Hi."

28.1 "Maybe" by The Three Degrees

28.2 Her voice is crazy. An alto voice. The voice of an occasional smoker. The organ holds a sermon behind her voice. The bass is true.

28.3 "I just fell all apart inside because I hadn't heard that voice in such a long time. I turned around…"

28.4 Hi, baby.

29. Next, "Bye."

29.1 "Don't Say Goodnight" by The Isley Brothers

29.2 We are approaching the end, and Mr. Yancey…

30. "Last Donut of the Night" is accurate if you believe this is the final track, and not the penultimate. There is a brief vocal sample early in the track, "A young man who went out and made a name for himself…" so goes a portion of the sample, but the most pertinent. Mr. Yancey—aka Jay Dee, aka J Dilla, aka Dilla, aka Dill Withers, aka the god (my nickname for him)—didn't attract me through his work with Slum Village who, I admit, I only tolerated until Mr. Yancey left the group, taking his beats with him. I hadn't thought much of Mr. Yancey until after his death. He produced some of my favorite music, including "Stakes Is High" by De La Soul, "Didn't Cha Know" by Erykah Badu, and while I blame

him for the disjointed sound of late-era A Tribe Called Quest, he blessed Q-Tip with a fire album, *Amplified,* as well as Common's *Like Water for Chocolate* and D'Angelo's *Voodoo.* At once boisterous and underrated, Mr. Yancey sat back in the shadows—a true beatmaker in that sense, one who understands his historical role in hip-hop—and this intrigued me. How can you be both unknown and famous? How can you be both prolific and hidden? How can you produce creative work, and have it consumed by thousands, yet still feel slept on? It seemed to me that, from life to death, Mr. Yancey created the music he loved, the music he wanted to hear in the world, and that his creative pursuit, no matter how altruistic to the community in whole, was singular in nature. I didn't cry when he died. Rather, I read about his passing online, on a shitty Dell laptop that contained a novel I would finish, but never revise, considered unworthy of the world, and in response to his death, I bought *Donuts*. I bought *Donuts* the way I now read Jenny Diski's essays in the *London Review of Books*. I don't want to know what impending death feels like—I can imagine—but I want to consume art colored by death. Because sooner or later, we're all going to die. Mr. Yancey was presented with a series of facts—an incurable blood disorder, with the addition of lupus, added up to a grim prognosis—and continued to work. I come back to *Donuts*, and consider it one of the best albums of the early 21st century, because it is unabashedly scared, and angry, and resigned: it is a black man on death's door, the heart of a boy in its final expression. Mr. Yancey, indeed extinct from our planet, was afforded a rare gift: time to prepare. And in preparation for his departure from our world, as he readied for his transition into the next world, after life, or into Nothingness—time will tell—Mr.

Yancey left us a final love letter. I don't recognize the posthumous releases. *Donuts* is the end. So now we close with the intro.

31. "Donuts (Intro)"

31.1 "When I Die"

31.2 "Not Available"

31.3 "Stay With me"

31.4 The primary vocal sample whines above the melody, an outstretched "be" elongated over time, connecting with "The kind of man that you thought I'd…" until Mr. Yancey's final message presents itself to us.

31.5 Shuggie Otis makes a reappearance, and the last track hooks into the first.

31.6 I imagine a circle.

32. James Yancey was born on February 7, 1974.

Footnotes:

1, 3, 4, 5: Aku, Timmhotep. "Fantastic Voyage." Stones Throw Records. April 5, 2006. http://www.stonesthrow.com/news/2006/04/fantastic-voyage.

2: Sanneh, Kelefa. "James Yancey, 32, Producer Known for Soulful Hip-Hop." The New York Times. February 14, 2006. http://query.nytimes.com/gst/fullpage.html?res=9D05EEDA123EF937A25751C0A9609C8B63.

BOILING SPRINGS ROCK CITY

by James Stafford

THE cool kid at Holden's Chapel Middle School was Chuck Morris. He had a dirt bike, never took a turn on the twirly slide, and flirted with Lisa Jacobson's mother every afternoon when she rolled up in her '55 Thunderbird. As the new kid in this small southern town, Chuck had everything that I aspired to.

He may have been the most popular fifth grader in Boiling Springs, but Chuck was too cool for everybody but the pretty girls and Brewer, whose dad owned the local nightclub. Each morning at recess, while the other kids flocked to the playground equipment and I sat by myself on the edge of the grass, Chuck and Brewer strolled coolly about and called each other Bo and Luke.

"Why do you guys call each other Bo and Luke?" I asked one morning.

"You know, Duke," Chuck said.

"Can I be Duke?"

He looked at me like I'd declared Potsie my favorite *Happy Days* character. "Duke is their last name. *Dukes of Hazzard.* Don't they have TVs up north?" That was the only conversation I had with Chuck during our entire fifth grade year.

Over the next year I shed my Yankee skin with a complete redneck makeover: Levi's, Army field jacket, black concert tees. I was no longer invisible to Chuck the Great; in fact, I was now the guy with whom Chuck spent his recess discussing music, motorcycles, and breasts.

"Where do you get your hair cut?" he asked.

"Gregory's Barber Shop."

"That's for old people! You should go to Jane's."

"That's where my Mom goes!"

"Have you ever seen Jane? She's a fox. When she cuts the back of your hair she stands in front of you."

"So?"

"So her boobs are in your face and she always wears sweaters. I touched one last time I got my haircut."

Jane administered the rest of my childhood haircuts.

Chuck's favorite motorcycle was the Honda Elsinore, which featured prominently in *On Any Sunday*, Bruce Brown's now legendary documentary about motorcycle racing, and also Chuck's favorite movie. While the other kids battled for the twirly slide, Chuck and I walked coolly around the playground, talking dirt bikes.

My twelfth birthday was coming up, so I asked my parents for an Elsinore and a birthday party. "I don't know, honey," my mother said. "Motorcycles are pretty dangerous. You can have a party, though."

"Can I have a sleepover?"

"Yes, but not too many boys," she sighed.

My only previous party was for my seventh birthday, and that one featured a Winnie the Pooh cake and a Mego Batman action figure who quickly lost his life to a garbage bag parachute and a power line. That kind of kid stuff wouldn't play at age twelve, especially not since I was best buds with the coolest kid in class. I needed ideas.

My big sister's boyfriend, Mike, was the epitome of big kid cool—I'd simply use him as a template for my big sleepover. Mike's room had no toys, just music, weights, and porn. Music and porn! This would be the greatest guy party of all time, and if I needed any more evidence that the universe was smiling upon me, a film entitled *Dirt* was in theaters. It wasn't *On Any Sunday*, but it was a documentary that featured off-road racing.

I invited every boy in the class, and I greased the tracks with a free movie, the complete KISS collection, and a stack of nudie magazines. Now all I needed to do was screw up the courage to ask Mike for a 24-hour loan of his porn stash. That never happened, but the party did and so did the motorcycle. It wasn't an Elsinore, but it was a Honda: A 1964 S65. I had a bike and friends—I wasn't an outsider in South Carolina anymore.

I even had an admirer: Serena, a newly arrived fellow

carpetbagger. She was even more of a misfit than I—skinny, loud, freckles, and had a helicopter mom who hyped her daughter's talents at every opportunity. Serena could sing and tap dance, act, knew ballet, on and on. She was funny and charming and cute and I didn't want to have anything to do with her because she was an outcast and for the first time I wasn't on the Island of Misfit Toys.

Aside from being chased around by Serena, sixth grade ended on a fairly high note. I spent my summer on my little motorcycle or swimming in the pond near our house. My neighbor, Rick, would come over and we'd get out the ladder and the baseball bats and air guitar to KISS records. "You're going to meet them someday," Rick said. "I just know it." Some afternoons we'd head into the woods with the neighborhood kids for epic games of kick the can. That summer was a bit like a Mark Twain novel, only with Atari, but I couldn't wait for seventh grade to start: junior high school, the big time.

• • •

Boiling Springs, South Carolina never tore down a high school, they simply repurposed them. The elementary school was the oldest of the decommissioned high schools. Holden's Chapel, my middle school for the past two years, was the former black high school. The junior high school was the most recent former high school, and as such it was fairly large. It housed grades seven through nine, and in a surprising turn to me was fed not only by my school but another elementary school. This meant a whole new group of kids and their respective cliques to deal with. I'd lived in the south for two years, but I was about to be a new kid again. Fortunately I had my buddy Chuck.

The Hendrix Elementary crowd had their own Chuck. His name was Danny, and they adored him. The girls fawned over him and the guys jockeyed to be near him. Both simple physics and comic book logic demanded that these two mighty forces either attract or repel each other. Would the two combine into a mutant, two-headed ultra-popular beast, or did Boiling Springs Junior High only have room for one hero? Perhaps one of the two was destined for life in a secret lair beneath the band room, where he would hatch schemes and occasionally send Grape Ape, his evil henchman, to terrorize the student body that rejected him.

But there would be no super villains: Chuck and Danny hit it off immediately. What a stroke of luck for me. Without even trying I was in orbit around the two biggest planets in the junior high solar system, but the trajectory of that orbit degraded rapidly. I didn't have the right clothes, the right shoes, the right friends (other than Chuck). I played baseball, not soccer. On and on, always in the form of little jokes punctuated with "I'm just kidding, man. You're cool."

One afternoon I caught up with Chuck and Danny just before math class. They were making a list.

"What are y'all doing?" I asked.

"We're working on our guest list," Danny said.

"Y'all are throwing a party?"

"Yeah, at Brewer's dad's club," Chuck said.

"When?"

"Next Friday night."

"This is going to be awesome! I'll bring some jams!"

Danny looked at Chuck, and then he wrote my name on the guest list.

Friday rolled around. Mike had taken lately to wearing a straw cowboy hat, its brim tightly creased. It looked really cool on him, so I asked to borrow it. Hat, Levi's, black t-shirt with a half buttoned flannel over it, and Nikes—I was styling. I grabbed my KISS albums and waited for a ride from my mother.

The party was packed, the dance floor jammed with girls shaking their developing butts to Kool and the Gang, Earth, Wind & Fire, and The Sugarhill Gang. "Rapper's Delight" was huge at the time, one of those monster hits that comes along every few years. The boys crowded the soda fountain at the waitress station. They were mixing suicides—the deadly mix of all available carbonated beverages that really just tastes kind of like Dr. Pepper. I thought the boys were idiots but I enjoyed watching them entertain each other, and I really liked watching the girls. I liked their monogrammed sweaters and their add-a-bead necklaces; I liked watching their Jordaches, Calvins, and Gloria Vanderbilts move to the music. They danced with each other because guys didn't dance. There wasn't a single guy within ten feet of the floor.

I found a table near the dance floor, pulled down the brim of my loaner cowboy hat, and ogled as subtly as I could.

Ogling quickly turned into observing. I can't very well liken it to an out-of-body experience, but it was the first out-of-room experience that I can remember. Almost 35 years later those moments persist. I'm seated at the back of a restaurant as I write this, as far to the back as I can possibly be. Behind me is the door to the office. I chose this seat. From here I can see the whole dining room like the set of an elaborate play, and I'm the only audience member.

Life bubbles around me. A Mexican couple is on a date at the next table, as is a handsome middle-aged couple sharing a pitcher of sangria. To my right is a four-top filled with Baby Boomers sounding off on the sorry state of the nation.

"February 3, 1967. I didn't take another sick day until 2003…"

"…I told him I saw him, but he didn't care. Just lazy…"

"…I liked it much better back then…"

The restaurant is loud. The voices blend into a drone. Occasionally one voice rises above the din and the dialogue bleeds into my scribbling.

"The point is I learned…"

"Anyway, there's several options…"

But I'm not here, not in this room. I'm in this notebook, in these ears, these eyes, watching. I'm still the boy sitting on the edge of the playground; the owl in the eaves, watching it all happen. I like it here.

And I liked it there, next to the dance floor with my stack of KISS records on the table beside me and my underdeveloped mind trying to sort out why the boys huddled together while the girls danced. I liked watching Serena dominate the dance floor with her years of lessons, all of those hours paid for by her helicopter mother coming back threefold here among the kids who shunned her daughter daily. Eventually the other girls sat down but Serena kept dancing. Chuck threw on Jay Ferguson's "Shakedown Cruise," his favorite at the time, in an attempt to shut her down. Serena kept dancing.

"You can't dance to that!" Chuck yelled.

"I can dance to anything!" she yelled back, and she never stopped moving.

Chuck ran to my table. It was the first time he'd talked to me all night. "Give me your hardest song," he said. I handed him *Destroyer.*

"Detroit Rock City," I said. "She can't dance to that." Chuck tucked it under his arm and ran back to the DJ booth. The song's opening montage filled the room: the rattling of breakfast dishes; a car door; an engine sparking to life; the tinny sound of an AM radio.

"What is this?" Serena asked.

Chuck pointed and laughed. "I thought you could dance to anything!" The other guys started laughing, too. Even the girls—the good little Southern Baptist girls—snickered behind their hands while Serena Behar stood alone on the dance floor. Then Ace's guitar faded in like some sort of 4/4 alarm*: na nah na nah na nah na nah na nah na nah.* Peter's drums came in with the classic rock beat*: boom bap boom boom bap / boom bap boom boom bap.* Serena was off, hitting it every bit as hard as if "Detroit Rock City" was "Le Freak." She shook the swan off her Gloria Vanderbilts. The other girls remained seated, but the boys flooded the dance floor. They struck their best air guitar poses, sang along with Paul, stuck their tongues out like Gene, flew their devil horns.

I wish I could say that I realized at that moment the lie that Serena inadvertently exposed. I wish I was hip enough then to realize that rock and roll was simply black music in white face, that rhythm was rhythm, that if there was a backbeat you could use it. That epiphany would take a few more years, though. That night I was satisfied with my newfound admiration for Serena, the girl whose crush I denied because she wasn't part of the in-crowd but who was actually cooler than all of us put together.

My other great epiphany of that evening was that I belonged on the periphery, that I enjoyed the role of observer. No, not enjoyed: I was an observer. It felt right sitting there alone watching the evening unfold. It was pleasurable, interesting, satisfying. I had no business in a cowboy hat. That suit of clothes simply didn't fit me. I was the camera eye, the secret recorder. I was the owl haunting the eaves.

"Having fun?" Chuck sat down across from me, pulling me out of the eaves and back to the table.

"Yeah, this is a great party."

Chuck looked at me, looked through me. "You know nobody wanted you here. You invited yourself," he said, and he tossed *Destroyer* onto my stack of records and walked away. I sat there for another twenty minutes waiting for my mother to arrive, very much in the room, very much alone.

DANCE OUTSIDE YOURSELF

by Khanisha Foster

AT Midnight, December 12, 2013 Beyoncé dropped a surprise album that rocked bodies all over the globe. Black women everywhere, we jumped on Facebook and Twitter declaring allegiance to our sexuality, our art, our partners and children—if we had them—and to our curvy ass bodies.

My curvy ass body, though, was getting ready to go to bed when #Beyoncé, #LifeMade, #goblackgirl began popping into my Twitter feed. I saw real-time video chats of people listening to the album in tears. And even though I was still mad at Beyoncé for not being funny in Austin Powers—some grudges are hard to let go of—I was intrigued. So I bought her album for two reasons:

1. Social media shut down the world when it dropped.
2. I had $78.99 worth of iTunes credit.

My body collapsed into my bright orange velvet chair. I clicked play with the intention of listening to one song. The first thing I heard was Harvey Keitel, Mr. White himself, asking: "Ms. Third Ward, your first question, what is your aspiration in life?"

And the silky dust of Beyoncé's voice replied, "My aspiration in life? To be happy."

Now, in 1985 when Beyoncé was four years old and starting to perform in local talent shows, I was five and both of my parents were heroin addicts.

There are lots of reasons why people self-medicate. One that both of my parents had in common was that they were both manic-depressive. This meant that when erratic joy entered my mom's eyes and crippling sadness entered my dad's I had a few fleeting moments of sobriety to get their attention. Even then, at five years old, I knew there was power in changing the subject, so I would perform every sketch I could remember from Saturday Night Live until they laughed so hard all they could think about was the next joke. It made me feel better, and it kept them from those extended escapes into the bathroom.

So when Queen B said, "To be happy," my husband Tony caught my eyes over the laptop screen, and I burst into tears.

I stayed up all night listening, considering the idea that the world could be filled with people trying to be happy, and I was changed. Or at least I was starting to change. Three of my Facebook posts from the week of the release prove it:

1. Pre-Download: *Wait, Beyoncé's new album has a Parental Advisory label… okay, let's do this.*

2. The next morning: *Facebook! Not saying it just to say it, Beyoncé changed music and the industry last night. I'm feeling like everything I love and struggle with as a woman/artist/mother/sexual being was thrown down, flipped, and reversed on that album. Mad respect.* (Side note: anyone who experienced that record with a partner that night knows why I didn't write that post until the next morning. We can say it right? We all had crazy amazing sex that night. Thank you Beyoncé!)

3. Two days later: *#NewYearsResolution to learn the dances in every Beyoncé video. This may also be my husband's Christmas present next year.*

This was not a throwaway statement on Facebook. It was, and it remains, A Radical Act of Joy. Some years come for you, and 2013 into 2014 was that for me. I lost my grandmother, two of my uncles, and my aunt, all in a two-month period. And then there was my dad. He had me on speakerphone, like always, and I could hear my step-mom, Karen, sniffling in the background.

He spoke directly: "You know, Karen didn't like the way he said it, but I appreciated the doctor's bluntness. You just gotta say these things. It's looking like cancer. How much is it gonna cost you to fly home? I'm gonna put that money in your account."

My dad and I don't have a relationship based on money. We've never even exchanged Christmas gifts. And the only birthday present he ever gave me came the year that I turned ten. He got sober. While that present is precious, it's also complicated because there are strings attached.

"You and your sister saved me," my father was fond of

saying. "If it wasn't for the two of you, I wouldn't be here." Which I always took to mean that I couldn't mess up because my dad's life depended on it.

• • •

In a tiny Chicago apartment I'm working on my first Beyoncé dance lesson with an instructor. I tried to teach myself, but when you don't like to mess up, trying to keep up with Beyoncé one-on-one can be humiliating. Kish is a friend from college. She's a bubbly sister naturally and the fact that she is in love adds to her glow. I know full well and good that I'm not going to dance like Beyoncé right away, but I am still struggling.

"Okay. Okay. I'm feeling it." Kish nods as we rewind "Flawless" and I leap along, trying to catch up.

A dancer since she was five, Kish rolls her shoulders forward with Queen B's stank face in perfect control, and then lets her booty lead her hips in a twist around. The booty I can do. I've got booty for days, but my shoulders are like a block of cement. It's from years of pulling them in when I don't want to feel sad. Sitting in prison visitation rooms waiting for my parents. Explaining to the other kids, "Yes that was my dad who got arrested at parent-teacher conferences." As the kid of an addict, you live with the knowledge that you will never be as important as the next high.

I tell Kish I need a glass of water. I need to give my shoulders a break. When she comes back in, I'm marking the second half of the dance. She sets the glass down next to a huge mirror.

"Have you noticed that you don't look at yourself when you dance? You just look at the floor."

Shoot. She called me on it. I spend a lot of time throwing the focus to other people. Growing up, I was in the practice of disappearing while my parents were the spectacle of every moment. Some days, especially after they got sober, I loved that about them. My dad in an Applebee's is like Samuel L Jackson in a diner in a Quentin Tarantino movie. The booth is his pulpit. I can remember him laying out some advice for me there when I was seventeen. I was focused on saving everybody else, even people that didn't need saving. I was telling my dad that one of my friends had shown up at my door blue and nearly unconscious after a night of drinking.

"I don't understand," I'd told him, crying. Since being a good girl was the greatest form of rebellion in my house.

"It's not your job to. You can't fix people, Khanisha. People are gonna be who they are. It's your job, oh, hold on, hold on—"

He waved the waitress over mid-sentence.

"Yeah, I want three Chocolate Malts, not milkshakes, malts. Bring me two now, one when the food comes, and I'll let you know if I need another one after we eat. Now where was I? Oh yeah. It's not your job, Khanisha. It's your job to create the life that you want to live. They'll either come around or they won't, but if they do, they going to need to see that they didn't take you down with them when they were at their darkest. Now, when the aliens come, I'm just glad you're going to be the one who's going to teach them about the world."

This is the dad that dominates my memories. The same guy who bench-pressed four hundred and fifty pounds on his fifty-fourth birthday just to prove he could. I never expected him to be the one who would disappear, but after a year of chemo trying to attack the cancer that was on his tongue and lymph nodes climbing down his throat, a year of eating nothing more then a protein shake a day, I could see the effects on his body. The collar of his usually tight triple XL shirt hung like a hula-hoop around his neck. His skin fell over his bones like sheets draped over furniture. I hugged him, and I felt like I'd crush him, but light took over the exhaustion in his eyes. He smiled and revealed that his teeth were now his most dominant feature as they were the only part of him that couldn't shrink. He quickly fell into a sob on my shoulder.

I'd never felt my father's bones press into me before, against my cheek, under my hands. He was sicker than I'd let myself believe. Delicate in a way that was hard to understand.

• • •

During the next dance session I hid my heartbreak pretty easily. I'm good at that. I pretended that the joy project was about the past and not the present. I felt the rhythm roll through my body with power, but the sequence of the steps seemed lost. How was I supposed to make space in my brain for order when my heart was so full of chaos?

But as Kish counted out loud in eights, my body took over. As my shoulders rocked forward and the cement softened I realized that this was not just a Radical Act of Joy, but a physical one. My body was on lockdown, hiding heartbreak in every crevice. And Beyoncé's body? That sister is thighs, hair, and freedom. The moves started to fall in order, and I was careful, trying to match Queen B's precision, when Kish said, "Great. You're doing the moves, now let me see you in it."

Kish catches everything.

I'd practice my dance after my morning phone calls to my dad. The deal I made with myself was that I could cry, but shortly after I had to replace my tears with sweat. Calling him every day wasn't a part of the cancer, it was just a part of our daily routine. We'd done it for twenty-three years, ever since he got sober, and we never missed a day. If one of us didn't pick up we'd rush to call the other back. He worried about my safety because I was his kid and I worried about his for obvious reasons.

It was three days before Mother's Day when he did not answer. It was two days before Mother's Day when I left the message: *Dad, are you okay? You didn't call me back. Hopefully you're just tired. Call me. I'm worried.*

It was the day before Mother's Day when my sister called me. I heard her breathing first.

"Sheridan?"

Nothing but her breathing again.

"Are you okay?"

"No. No." (Breath) "I'm not. It's Dad."

I sat on the bed and waited in her pause. I readied myself for sadness.

"Dad is using again."

It was a white-hot anger that came instead.

• • •

Sheridan described how my step-mom had found him, but I already knew what it looked like. I was five again, walking into the bathroom to find my dad sitting on the closed toilet in tighty whities, a tan rubber cord wrapped around his bulging brown arm. His veins swollen, especially the one with the needle sticking out of it. His closed eyes, his breath drawing his chin up towards the ceiling. On the pink swirled counter just beyond him: tin foil, a spoon, his orange plastic Bic lighter, and his open black duffel bag on the floor. The way he didn't see me there.

The only difference was that then he had a body to give. Then, he'd been protected by muscle and youth, but now all he had was skin and bones and two metal hips. I was not surprised, because you cannot be the child of an addict and be surprised. But I was lost. Who was I if not the little girl who had saved her dad from himself? I still wanted to save him, so I started our phone calls again and every day I would say: "I love you dad."

And every day we would go through some version of this:

"What? What? What are you talking about? What happened?"

"I love you dad."

My step-mom would say over the speakerphone, "I don't know what to say, ten thousand of our savings is missing, so…"

"I love you dad."

"Look if you cared for me you would call me more, this wouldn't have happened in the first place if you loved me."

"I love you dad."

"I don't need you. I got family. Real family."

"I… love you dad."

"I'm sorry, Niti. I never should have said those things to you. Not you."

"I love you dad."

"Look, I'm, uh, I'm sorry. I'm gonna get tested regularly. The doctor said there's a link you can check with the results. I just want you to trust me again."

"I love you dad."

And then he got high again.

And I stopped.

I stopped calling.

Because I was hearing two voices: the one on the other end of the phone and the one from my memories.

"It's not your job, Khanisha. They need to see that they didn't take you down with them. Keep yourself safe."

All those years, he wasn't preparing me for the world, or for the aliens. It was him. He was warning me about himself.

• • •

I kept practicing the dance. Practicing turning my tears into sweat. Practicing because I didn't want to have the kind of sadness that made my children responsible for my laughter.

So I rolled my shoulders. And I twisted my hips. And I rolled my shoulders. And I twisted my hips. But those little pockets of my body I'd been hiding in—they wouldn't move—they wouldn't shift.

And Kish was looking at me and I was looking at the floor again and she said, "Khanisha, dance outside yourself."

My skin tingled, trying to hold it all in. My chin floated up. My gaze opened out. The back beat dropped and—CRACK. The room couldn't hold me. My body was an exorcist and pain was the poltergeist. I stirred every bit of chaos with my ass. And, naw, I wasn't the little girl who saved her daddy. I was a beast. With each hip grind I devoured joy and spun it new again. I was freedom, and I didn't even need the hair and the thighs, cause I was floating above. I didn't have a body to be held down in. I was outside.

ME & IGGY & JOHN

by Troy Palmer

I was already feeling a little out of place in the line-up. John and I seemed like the youngest Iggy Pop fans there, if you could even call John a fan. It didn't help when he turned to me in a bit of a panic as the line began to move forward, inching us closer to The Godfather of Punk.

"Oh man. I didn't bring anything for him to sign. Do you have something I could borrow, bud?"

"Sorry. I only have my stuff."

John thought about it for a second and then came up with an idea.

"Hey, maybe I can get him to sign my parole papers."

• • •

John is an old, close friend. We grew up together in the public housing projects of South Oshawa, a dying blue-collar town just outside of Toronto, and we were thick as thieves, literally. Our neighborhood, know as "The Hill" by those who lived there and those who didn't, wasn't a terribly violent place, but it was one that you didn't want to spend much time in, just to be on the safe side.

Criminals, alcoholics, white-trash guys who beat their kids / wives / pets, me and John, and our small group of tight-knit friends. This was home.

Our friendship formed quickly and easily the summer before Grade 8. All it took was for one of us to say or do something stupid and goofy and for the other one to think it was the funniest fucking thing in the world. It was a bond formed almost instantly. From then and all through high school, we would continue make each other laugh with made-up raps, stupid gags, and practical jokes. We'd listen to new music in my room, play Dungeons and Dragons on Saturday afternoons, and have go-nowhere crushes on the same girls. And we would pick up the not-so-innocent hobby of car hopping.

Summer nights we would venture into neighboring parking lots and let ourselves into unlocked cars to steal spare change and lighters, see what bad music people were listening to. If we didn't like your choice of Linda Rondstadt or the Oak Ridge Boys, we'd take your cassettes and throw them into the nearest dumpster. I viewed it as a public service.

For me, this was something to pass the time. There was an

adrenaline rush that came with the close calls of getting caught. It was exhilarating and it felt like no one got hurt. But the more we did it, the more John wanted to do. Why stop at unlocked cars? Why stop at spare change? Why stop at cars?

Things changed the night we lifted a guy's checkbook from his glove box. A checkbook filled with all kinds of information we never expected to happen upon: an account number, a balance, a name, and a signature.

I spent the next couple of days locked in my bedroom, practicing how to sign the guy's name. I did it over and over until John and I felt it was close enough—close enough that we could walk into the bank and get ourselves a few extra bucks. That was the plan. But by the time we got around to actually attempting this, we had convinced ourselves that to make the risk worthwhile, we should probably try to get more than just a few extra bucks. We wanted it all.

This was at a time when people still had to actually go into the bank—it wasn't some simple ATM scam. It was live and in person. And in retrospect, completely fucking insane. In the bank, I filled out a withdrawal slip for most of the money in the guy's account, leaving a couple of bucks behind to avoid suspicion. I gave the slip to the teller and signed it as steadily as I could in front of her. I could feel my heart in throat, though I wasn't sure it was even still beating. John sat in a chair by the window, doing his best to not look like he was waiting for the only other public housing kid in the bank. He might have even been reading a paper. And he wore sunglasses. This I remember, because it made him seem more prepared than I was for what we were attempting. The teller started the transaction but wisely began asking me some questions—just standard things, but I wasn't prepared for them at all. Then she moved away from her window and went to speak with who I'm guessing was her manager and one other person who my brain would only let me assume was some type of plainclothes security. I decided the best move for me to make as my next one was to get the fuck out of there. I stepped away calmly, giving John as small a signal as I could when I walked past him. He got up behind me and we strolled out the front door. Once we cleared the bank's wall of windows, I told John to run. And we ran like hell.

And with that, I was done. The rush of what was essentially an attempted bank robbery was more than enough for me.

But my finish line turned out to be John's starting point. From there, he started hanging out with people who were more willing accomplices and who were either smarter criminals or dumber friends than I was. After upping his stealing game, he got into a bit of trouble and ended up in juvy. We speculated that it was his mom and step-dad who had turned him in.

When he escaped a couple of months into his time there, I was the person he came to. (Incidentally, he wasn't the first friend of my mine who came straight to me after running away from the law. I knew all too well about the trouble that would come my way, so I told John I couldn't help him and suggested he should just turn himself in.) He was free for about a day before he ended up going back. And sometime around then, he got into drugs.

By the time he got out legitimately, he was a marginally better criminal. His drug use turned into drug selling. And his drug selling turned into an ill-planned scheme of ripping off his customers. Selling them short. Selling them fake shit. It's the kind of behavior that can catch up with a guy, and when it caught it up with John it didn't end well.

He was never much of a scrapper, but he was strong and rangy. And John knew a desperate situation when he was in one. So when one of his buyers—a lifelong biker—grabbed him, John fought back as best he could.

I never got the full details of what happened—partly because John was too high, too scared to remember them—but it ended with John running away and the other guy face down in a creek, unconsciously breathing mouthfuls of water into his lungs until he died.

John's prison time wasn't easy. The guy who died at his hands had a lot of friends in prison and a son who deliberately got himself arrested, smashing up a row of parked cars in downtown Oshawa in attempt to get at John himself. After too many beatings at one prison, they would transfer John to another.

When he got released after serving the bulk of his five-year sentence for manslaughter, John was sent to live in a halfway house in Toronto. I was the only person he knew who lived in the city and we had kept in touch during his time away, writing to each other whenever we could. At one point he sent me a picture of how much upper body muscle he had put on. The once scrawny, lanky kid looked like he had swapped one addiction (drugs) for another (weights). Another time, he wrote to me about finding God. When I wrote him back, I told him told him I was happy he found something to believe in, but that maybe organized religion wasn't all it was cracked up to be. It was a while before he wrote me back again.

When we re-connected in person, it didn't take long for us to pick up where we left off before all the bad shit happened. He wasn't the same guy, of course—he had stopped drinking and doing drugs, but mostly he was a lot bigger and not used to being free. Despite the changes in him, we could still make each other laugh in ways that few others could even understand.

After being out for a little while, he got a part-time job and made plans to enroll in university. Bit by bit, his life was beginning to look like something normal (tagging along with his nerdy music friend to meet Iggy Pop at Tower Records aside).

• • •

"Hey, maybe I can get him to sign my parole papers."

"I don't know, John. I don't think that's such a good idea."

"No, it's okay. They expire soon and I'll get new ones."

I thought about what else I could offer him, but all I had with me were two copies of a book I had written. A book that had a hand-written letter from Iggy Pop on the back cover.

That was the reason we were there. Or at least the reason I was there. John just joined me at the last minute, forgetting what I had been telling him and everyone else I knew for weeks—that when Iggy came to town for an autograph session, I was going to be there. No matter what.

When Iggy's *American Caesar* came out in 1993, it caught me at a low point. Songs like "Hate," "Jealousy," and "Fuckin'

Alone" were like anthems to me at the time.

I was twenty. My father had been dead for two years and I had been re-playing his death daily ever since.

Instead of going to college or university, or otherwise getting on with my life, I was working at a semi-fast food place, flipping burgers for a living, trying to convince myself that the music and stories I was writing were worth something.

The job required me to wear a blue hat, a blue apron, and a white t-shirt with the restaurant's logo. For some reason a place called Blueberry Hill had a rainbow in their logo, so that was part of my grease-covered uniform as well—a rainbow. It wasn't the sexiest look for a skinny, awkward music nerd, as proven by the many cute university girls who passed through the restaurant with their sympathetic smiles of pre-emptive rejection aimed in my direction. They weren't the only ones who passed through and left scars. There were grown men and women who took great personal offense when I told them that cheese on their burger would cost an extra seventy-five cents. And there were party kids and club-goers and punks and jocks who banged on the window after hours to point and laugh at the greasy kid in his rainbowed t-shirt mopping the floors. I was on the wrong side of humanity's fishbowl.

Every night, I would come home to my creaky bachelor apartment. It was the first time I had lived on my own—like totally on my own—no roommates, no pets. (Though shortly after this time, I would adopt Casey, a lovely little cat named after the then-girlfriend of Jane's Addiction's Perry Farrell.)

The room was furnished with cheap and broken objects

that I took with me from one move to the next, clinging to them as if they were keeping me from floating away. They were the leftovers of my parents' marriage and my dad's life: a mattress and box spring, a dresser, some bed sheets, two end tables, and a massive, though no longer working, 1970s stereo cabinet (complete with a turntable, 8-track player and built-in storage for a handful of records and chunky, outdated cassettes). My working stereo, also with a turntable—but with dual cassette decks in place of the 8-track—sat on top of the old-school cabinet. It was a bottom-of-the-line blue light special from Kmart that I'd had since I was sixteen. I asked my dad for that stereo over and over, until he eventually surprised me with it that Christmas. Less than two years later, he went into the hospital because he wasn't feeling well. And less than a month after that—three days before what would have been his fiftieth birthday—he died of cancer.

In the liner notes for *American Caesar*, Iggy Pop put his mailing address and an invitation to write to him. So I did.

I sent him a story about a guy who flipped burgers for a living and who generally felt pretty shitty about himself. The story talked about how one day this guy walked into Record Peddler in Toronto (RIP) and bought Iggy Pop's *American Caesar*. And how on his way home to listen to the record, he remembered that he actually had to work that night at his generally shitty job. So he turned himself around, went into work and somehow every awful little thing that happened that night—that happened every night—didn't seem to matter. Not the pretty out-of-reach girls, not the grown ups who blamed him for the inflated price of cheese, not the jocks or the punks or the bros who all laughed at the greasy kid behind the counter. None of it. Because he knew that when he got home, he had Iggy's brand new record waiting for him. And it was going to be awesome.

I don't remember how much time passed, but one day I got a letter in the mail. It was handwritten on letterhead from a hotel in Malaysia:

Troy –

I think you write pretty fucking good. Don't be too proud to write for the market — I mean, find one that's available & produce for it — whether it's the local weather report, book reviews, or horror, or whatever. Just getting started is important. I'm 46, digging what's goin' on around me, excited to continue. Working's been good, gotta learn to relax, feel lucky. That's me for now.

Flip me a burger,

Iggy Pop

Holy. Shit.

He actually wrote me back. And even read my story.

With an Iggy-like energy, I got to writing. A few months later, I self-published a rather cathartic book of short stories and essays called *Immaculate Misconception*. Not having any connections to get the book blurbed, I decided to put Iggy Pop's hand-written letter on the back cover. I think I sold one copy. The rest I just gave away.

And I was there at Tower to give one to Iggy.

• • •

John pulled the parole papers from the front pocket of his jeans.

"I don't know, John. I don't think that's such a good idea."

"No, it's okay. They expire soon and I'll get new ones."

"Yeah, I don't know, man," I said.

But it didn't matter what I said or what I thought—the gleam in John's eye told me he was convinced. And with that, we made our way up the line.

John went first.

The signings up to this point had seemed to go in pretty much the same pattern: a fan walks up, puts something in front of Iggy, he listens, signs, makes a bit of eye contact and they're done. When John went up, the pattern changed. From my on-deck circle place in line, I watched as John put his stapled and creased parole papers in front of Iggy. Iggy looked at them, trying to decipher what exactly he was looking at. I could see John's mouth moving in profile, but couldn't make out what he was saying. Iggy looked up, still a bit unsure but listening intently. He looked back down at the papers, then up again at John. Then, he stood—bolted up out of his chair the way you would for a standing ovation following an artist's performance of lifetime, when you know you've just witnessed something epic, life-affirming. Only instead of breaking into applause, he wrapped his sinewy, legendary arms around John and proclaimed, loud enough for the back of the line to hear, *"Right fucking on, man."* Or something to that effect. He sat back down, newly inspired, and began to scribble and scrawl feverishly.

When he finished, he handed the papers back to John, gave him another hug and they shared another, quieter exchange. On the other side of the table, parallel to my position in the front of the line, was a small gathering of local reporters and photographers. As I moved toward the table for my turn at the man, my moment, my time, I found my head on a permanent swivel, watching as the reporters immediately formed a scrum around John. I could hear them asking questions on top of one another, could see the flash from the cameras in the corner of my eye.

Turning my attention back to Iggy, I began telling him how I wrote him a story and how he wrote me back and how I used that letter to blah blah blah blah blah. I could feel it myself. I'd been upstaged at my own show. I handed him a copy of the book and he said something along the lines of "Hey cool, thanks." And then someone tugged me by the elbow and escorted me stage left. The exit. I walked past John, still answering questions. The reporters all laughing and smiling along with him.

When we finally left, John showed me what Iggy had given him. Under the *Conditions of Parole* section—which included strict instructions to not consume alcohol or drugs or have a firearm—Iggy had written DO NOT ASSOCIATE WITH IGGY POP and he drew a stick figure behind bars, pleading for clemency, as best as a stick figure could. It was fucking awesome.

On the rest of the walk home, we talked about that moment, the reporters, Iggy. It took a while before John asked how it went with me.

"Good," I said in a tone that was meant to convince me as much as it was him.

The next day, John and I were grabbing some takeout from a Chinese restaurant around the corner from where I lived. As we waited for our Specials #2 and #3, I flipped open the paper. In the bottom corner of the front page of the entertainment section was a brief story of a young man who brazenly asked Iggy Pop to sign his probation papers. John grinned ear to ear as he ripped out the page and pocketed it. The article didn't name John, but it didn't have to.

• • •

In the months that followed, John and I would grow apart again. I would go back to school to study advertising, following Iggy's advice of learning to write for the market. John would fall back in with some other guys that we'd grown up around. The drinking buddy types. I would see him sporadically, like the time he showed up at a new place I was living at in the middle of winter, wearing just a t-shirt and jeans. He was there to ask if he could use my address for his welfare checks—something about his roommate's address being blacklisted by the system. I told him I couldn't do it, but I did send him back out into in the frigid Toronto night with a bomber jacket. He had lost most of the weight he'd put on in prison, but the coat was still at least one size too small. A couple of years after that, we spent an impromptu New Year's Eve together at my place. He would meet my future wife and I would meet his girlfriend at the time. It was a good night. She seemed good for him and he seemed happy. But like most of his life that preceded that night, the happy times wouldn't last. John would continue down that familiar path—that high wire of addiction and recovery, trouble and calm. His addictions eventually proved to be too much for his patient girlfriend and she eventually turned him over to his parole officer, sacrificing their relationship to try to get John the help he once again needed.

Last I had heard, John ended up back at his mom's house, close to where we grew up, and was working for a local landscaping company. That was over ten years ago. I don't know what his life is like now, but to steal some words from Iggy's letter, I hope John's learning to relax, feel lucky. And I hope that whenever he hears an Iggy Pop song, he thinks back to that day at Tower Records and remembers it the way I do. To steal some more words from Iggy, it was pretty fucking good.

STOP READING AND LISTEN

by Megan Stielstra

1.

Just after we eloped and just before the housing market crashed, my husband and I bought a condo across the street from the Aragon Ballroom. If you've never had the pleasure, the Aragon is a legendary music club on Chicago's North Side. Take the Red Line to the Lawrence stop in Uptown and it's the first thing you'll see: breathtaking (albeit crumbling) Spanish architecture, enormous light-up marquee, the line to get in wrapping into the alley, and ticket scalpers on every corner. Here's a fun game: find the nearest Chicagoan and ask them to tell you their Aragon story. Most of us [1] have one or two or five, and many of them go something like this: "Passed out at Rage Against the Machine," "Got peed on at Faith No More," "Broke my arm at Megadeth," "Lots of dudes whipping their penises around in circles at

Butthole Surfers;" [2] Profoundly dangerous and/or masochistic crowd surfing and/or mosh pit at KMFDM and/or Deadmau5 and/or Insane Clown Posse, and the classic: "Kicked in the face during Slayer. It was *awesome.*"

But there's more, of course.

There's always more.

So the story(ies) go(es): Capone had underground tunnels running between the Aragon and his favorite bar in Uptown: the Green Mill; good for bootlegging, good for hiding out from the cops, good for those massive secret parties that you always see in movies starring Leonardo DiCaprio. Back then, the Aragon was a ballroom dance hall housing one of the best orchestras in the country; Sinatra played there, as did Tommy Dorsey, Glenn Miller, and Lawrence Welk. Tuxedos and semi-formal—expected. The jitterbug—prohibited. In 1958, a fire next door caused extensive damage, and instead of bouncing back to its former Big Band glory, the Aragon became, in quick succession: a roller rink, a boxing arena, and a discotheque. Then, in the '70s, it housed these crazy, day-long, drunken, furious monster rock shows, thus earning its current nickname of "The Brawlroom" (ball/brawl—see what they did there?). And that, my friends, brings us roaring into the present: mid-sized rock tours, local Spanish language shows, and the occasional boxing match.

You can feel the history in this place. It's peeling off the walls with the paint.

2.

I don't know why I bought a condo. The American Dream, I guess. Adulthood. I used the phrase "building equity" a lot, although I wasn't entirely sure what it meant.

3.

I do know why I bought *that* condo. It was because of Jane's Addiction. In high school, I was a huge Jane's Addiction fan—still am, but adult devotion is nothing compared to teenage obsession. Fifteen-year-old me had walls papered in *Nothing's Shocking* posters. Fifteen-year-old me brought up Perry Farrell while discussing the great American poets in AP English class. Fifteen-year-old me made out with boys who wore eye makeup.

Thirty-eight-year-old me drinks Cabernet and plays "I Would For You" on repeat.

In November 1990, Jane's Addiction played a somewhat infamous show at the Aragon. At the time, I was a sophomore in high school in small town Southeast Michigan—no way in hell would I have been allowed to go to a concert in Chicago—but I had a sort-of boyfriend who was a few years older (shhhhhh, don't tell my dad) (hi, Dad!), and he made the four-hour drive to be there in his Ford Escort fueled by pop cans we meticulously collected and turned in to the grocery store for ten cents per. "It was awesome!" he told me the next day, his eyes still glazed from no sleep and the glory of the rock. "Perry Farrell climbed the walls! He was up there on the ceiling like a vampire! Everybody was throwing beer bottles, and smashing chairs, and full-body slamming into each other; it was so totally insane, like somebody *must* have died! There's no *way* somebody didn't die!"

"What about the music?" I said.

He looked at me like I was crazy and said, "That *was* the music."

Fifteen-year-old me didn't have much experience with live shows [3] [4]. I hadn't felt the high that comes from *being* there, being *part of it*—the collective energy of the shared experience. My sort-of boyfriend explained it via Star Trek: "It's like the Borg— we're thinking and moving and feeling as one," which in retrospect is a pretty fucked-up metaphor, what with their mass assimilation and "*resistance is futile*" and nanoprobes injected into your neck, but at the time?—I totally understood what he meant.

"You can't *get* it unless you're *in* it," he said, and that's how I wound up in the audience for the first ever Lollapalooza tour. It was August 4th, 1991, a few days before my sixteenth birthday. That summer, I'd been at an eight-week theater program at sleepaway camp—yeah, I said it, *sleepaway camp*—and for some reason my parents gave me permission to spend the day at the Pine Knob Amphitheater [5] in Clarkston, Michigan. I remember bits and pieces, a fast-changing montage of image and sound: Siouxsie and the Banshees, Nine Inch Nails, Ice-T; Butthole Surfers (no swinging dicks, FYI) and Living Color. Color! Wild clothes. Tattoos and piercings and mohawks, none of which I'd seen before. It rained for a bit; thousands of people danced in the mud. It was the first time I heard Henry Rollins, who performed his set with his back to the crowd, bent at the waist, and singing into a hand-held mic with his head between his knees. When the

Violent Femmes played, the entire audience sang along to that part in "Kiss Off" that goes, "and ten, ten, ten, ten for everything, everything, everything!"

Later, after the sun set over the main stage, people lit bonfires across the lawn, and Jane's Addiction took the stage. The sort-of boyfriend had splurged for pavilion tickets; [6] in my memory I can see the band's buttons and sweat and guitar strings. The night was warm and perfect. I remember standing on my seat. I remember screaming my head off. I remember dancing and not caring what I looked like while I danced—a freedom I haven't felt in decades. The song I most wanted to hear, "Summertime Rolls," was the third one they played that night, and when I heard its lilty, steamy opening bassline, I felt—

Maybe you'll think I'm corny as hell, but what I felt was joy.

This was the one I played over and over, alone in my bedroom on a scratched CD. This was the one I listened to when I fell asleep at night. This was *my* song—the one that spoke directly to *me*—and here I was with fifteen thousand people who felt the same way. Fifteen thousand people, all of us singing.

Me and my girlfriend

Don't wear no shoes

Her nose is painted pepper

Sunlight

She loves me

I mean it's serious

As serious can be…

Fifteen thousand people—fifteen *thousand*—all sharing the same moment.

Can you hear it?

Stop reading and listen.

4.

I moved to Chicago in 1995 after detours in Boston and Florence, Italy, that were admittedly ill-conceived (why did I go to that college? Why did I go to that country? Why do we do any of the crazy things we do?), but ultimately pretty great insofar as learning about the world and myself—coming of age and whatnot. I was dying to go to the Aragon, to stand inside the place where Perry Farrell had climbed the walls, but I'd only just turned twenty—still a year before I could legally get in. Somewhere during that time, my roommate started dating a guy who lived on the same block of Lawrence Avenue, and long story short: while the two of them hung out, I'd lean against the side wall of the Aragon and listen to the shows.

Weezer. Ozzy Osbourne. Reverend Horton Heat. Lenny Kravitz. Alanis Morrisette circa *Jagged Little Pill.*

It was *awesome.*

It was also, as I've been told on multiple occasions, stupid. Uptown had a reputation, then and still, for gang activity. It's also home to support services for many who are mentally ill. Also: lots of bars, which means lots of drunks. So why was a girl like me, young and alone and naive as hell, standing on a street corner in a place like Uptown? [7]

I never thought of it as a street corner. I thought of it as a rock concert.

More often than not, after I turned 21 and started going to shows *inside* the Aragon, I'd pretend that I smoked so I could go back out. On warm nights—cold ones, too; it's hot in there and there's no A/C—they throw open the windows, and the music bleeds into the air. I'd lean against the east side of the club, facing Winthrop, and feel the speakers vibrate through the ground and into my shoes. No one elbowed me in the jaw. No one dumped $2 PBRs down my shirt. Inevitably, I'd stare at the building across the street, with its crumbling yellow brick, its iron balconies, its turret. *I want a turret someday,* I'd think.

Two decades and 6.25% financing later, I had that very one.

5.

Recently, I was doing some work in a coffee shop, and at the next table I overheard a conversation between a young couple and their relator about the condo they'd just viewed. How it was everything they'd dreamed of and more. I wanted to lean over and say, Hi. Excuse me, sorry to interrupt, but you know that dreams change, right? And markets—they change, too. And sometimes the developer fucks up the roof to the tune of hundreds of thousands of dollars, and when they rig the building's electricity the wires stretch across your neighbors' backyard and they try to charge you to *rent their air* and lawsuitlawsuitlawsuit and yeah, sure, fine, at the beginning you can afford the mortgage on you and your husband's four jobs, but property taxes go up, and assessments go up, and you have to fix the roof, and you get pregnant, and the market crashes, and maybe you get sick, maybe you have a tumor or some shit, so you and your husband work more—you add more teaching gigs 'cause that's what adjuncts do and he signs on to a cubical job that slowly, over eight years, drains him like an I-fucking-V but hey, it's the American fucking way, right! and you're so, so lucky to have the jobs and so, so lucky to have the insurance and so, so lucky to have this beautiful, healthy little kid bouncing off the walls and your poor, kind neighbors downstairs [8] are so patient with the bouncing and the banging and the jumping, but still, you're saying, "Baby, don't jump," like nine hundred times a day and is that the parent you thought you'd be? and one time, the time that lives in your memory as The Last Straw, you open the closet door and squirrels jump out and go running around your living room and your kid's like, YAY SQUIRRELS! and you're like OMG RABIES! and people, as you sit here with your relator talking about dreams and imaginary numbers, my question is this: have you really thought this through? I mean *really?* Not the "We hooked up, moved in together, got a dog, got married and now we're supposed to buy a place 'cause that's the American Dream" sort of thing, because what if that dream *changes?* What if that dream is *changing*, right now, this moment, a plot-point on our historical timeline about privilege and ownership and societal norms and *do you really want to buy this condo?* I mean, far be it from me in the safety of hindsight to tell you what you should and should not do but man, if I could yell back across time to my younger self, I'd tell her, Honey—

Rent. [9]

6.

But hey—focus on the good, right? Here's what was good about that condo across the street from the Aragon:

1) My son was born there.

2) My neighbors were awesome.

3) Turret!

4) Sitting on that balcony, three stories above street level, listening to shows. On warm nights, they throw open the windows and the music, suddenly free of the four walls containing it, explodes into the streets. Makes me think of Pandora's Box: all that fury and rawness and savagery and hope hitting the air and becoming our breath. God, I loved it out there. Instead of $2 PBRs, I could pour a glass of wine. Instead of taking an elbow to the jaw, I'd eat popsicles with my kid and tell him about the bands.

"Who's playing tonight?" he'd ask.

"Megadeth," I'd say.

"Death is a band?"

"The Flaming Lips," I'd say.

"We don't lick the stove."

"The Pixies," I'd say.

"Pixies have glitter dust in their butts."

On that balcony, we heard Kim Deal play the opening notes of "Debaser" during the Pixies' 2009 *Doolittle* 20th anniversary tour. We heard LCD Soundsystem do "Daft Punk Is Playing At My House." We heard Morrissey, Johnny Cash, M.I.A., and a gazillion others.

7.

During the years we lived across from the Aragon, I stopped being a part of the audience. Instead, I watched them. Up there, I had a front row seat.

When Rob Zombie played, his crowd refused to leave. They mobbed the street, blocking traffic both ways down Lawrence Avenue, chanting "*ZOMBIE! ZOMBIE!*" (I wish they'd been talking about actual zombies. That would've been awesome). Some guy who used to play with The Grateful Dead headlined a show, and forgive the generalization, but the whole neighborhood had a contact high. I remember when the show let out at 2 a.m., and we woke up to a wicked ten-guy pile-up in the street. This happened a lot: the fighting and yelling and drunken brawls; the punching and swearing and bloody noses. But this was the first time everyone involved was wearing tie-dye. My husband opened the window and yelled, "Aren't you guys supposed to love each other?" Kid Rock's fans backed away when they saw him, parting like the Red Sea as he walked the block from his limo to the front door. President Obama had his 50th birthday party at the Aragon, and the Secret Service wouldn't let us leave our building.

When they filmed the club scene in *Public Enemies*, they wrapped a chain-link fence around the block to protect Johnny Depp from screaming women. When the Yeah Yeah Yeahs played, I couldn't get off the L. When Weezer played, I couldn't get off Lakeshore Drive. The week I came home from the hospital with my new baby, born three weeks early in the middle of a snowstorm, Marilyn Manson played.

His audience broke a tree in front of my building.

They broke a *tree*. [10]

8.

I'm interested in audience. How we come together, feel the high of *being* there. For years, I wrote mainly for live performance; specifically, live performance in bars. The audience is *right there*. So is the laughter, the gasps, and blank faces if I've lost them. When I sit down to write, that's what I'm imagining: the connection, the energy, and the collective electricity of joy or shock or empathy.

The essay was first named by Michel de Montaigne as "Essais," which means "attempts." I like that—an attempt. Here's my attempt to try out an idea. Here's my attempt to figure out what I think. Here's my attempt to show you what I've seen, and to share that experience with you. Sometimes, those experiences are fun; the wild and the edgy, the young and the stupid and the free.

But there's more to the story.

There's always more.

9.

Yelling and fighting at 2 a.m., immediately followed by gunshots. My husband called 9-1-1, and we watched out the window 'til the sirens came; first police, then fire trucks, then an ambulance. Our bedroom was filled with red and blue light. A small crowd collected on the sidewalk next to the Aragon, and later, we'd find out a teenage boy had died. I wish I could say it was the first time it had happened. I wish I could say it was the last.

An hour later—quiet now, and dark—I got back into bed and began the tricky, foggy work of talking myself back into sleep. I don't know how long I was out before the crying started. No, not crying, that word's too weak; this was a wail. A male voice, wailing. Low and desperate and destroyed, deep at the base of his throat. Maybe at first, I dreamt it, but soon I was sitting up, fully awake, and back to the window.

Three stories below, the boy's father stood where his son had been shot. He stood there all morning—3 a.m., 4 a.m., 5 a.m.—and the whole time, he wailed. A single, raw sob; a few of beats of silence; then another. It made me think of contractions—the pause between the pain. My husband and I sat on the bed, wide awake and listening. We sat there in all of our privilege: our newborn son alive and healthy and asleep in his tiny turret bedroom; our safe, warm home; our middle class upbringings and middle class lives, our education and jobs and insurance; our families; our skin color; our faith; all of it so enormous and so puny in the face of all that pain. I considered reaching into the nightstand to grab the little foam earplugs I used sometimes when the Aragon opens its windows because sometimes the noise is too much, the music and the traffic and the violence and the loss. It's easier to drown it out, to change the channel, to read something else, to believe the same old story, to stick my fingers in my ears and say *Lalalalala* instead of listening to a grief I couldn't fathom and the truths in the world that I don't want to see.

I sat there, listening.

I imagined people awake, listening, up and down the block. Awake, listening, all across Uptown. Awake, listening, across the city, maybe the country.

Are you awake? Can you hear it?

Stop reading and listen.

10.

Just after we had a baby and just before we could no longer afford our mortgage, I passed a woman and her daughter standing in front of the Aragon. The mom was in her mid-forties, in Capri pants and a sweatshirt that said GAP. She clutched her purse in both hands and stared up at the Aragon. Her eyes were wide. Her mouth was dropped open. I think she may have gasped. I remembered the first time I saw the Duomo in Florence, or the Fred and Ginger house in Prague, how tiny I felt in the face of all that beauty, all that history—and I looked up at the Aragon, too. I'd been living across from it for nearly three years. It had become part of my every day, and I couldn't remember the last time I really *saw* it.

What a mind-blowingly beautiful building. Mosaic tilework lines the walls, with concrete vines running up to sculpted faces that sometimes smile and sometimes frown. In its day, this place was the most famous dancehall in the country, packing in eighteen thousand people a week. Eighteen *thousand.* It survived prohibition. It survived the Great Depression. Lawrence *Welk* played there. So did B.B. King. So did The Doors, The Kinks. And Jane's Addiction in 1990, when I wasn't much older than the girl standing next to me on the sidewalk.

She was fourteen, maybe fifteen, and in that painful, awkward vortex of *OMG gross I'm with my mom.* Too much foundation over acne scars. Too much Abercrombie & Fitch. Too-huge headphones jutting out like Princess Leia buns. She held an iPhone in front her face—texting, maybe? YouTube?—and was completely oblivious to her mother, the Aragon, me watching the both of them, and all of Uptown surrounding us: people rushing to work, traffic rushing by, colored chalk pictures on the sidewalk, pigeons pooping on every damn thing, the L train thundering above, radios with the bass turned all the way up, dogs and kids and runners and commuters. And three stories above us, in the yellow brick building across the street, my newborn son was fast asleep in his turret.

The mom nudged her.

She glanced up.

The mom spun her fingers by her ears—the universal gesture for *take off the goddamn headphones.*

The daughter rolled her eyes, but she did it.

The mom put one arm around her (*puke, OMG gross*) and held out the other like she was going to hug the building. "This," she announced, "is the Aragon Ballroom." Her voice held a profound sort of awe, as if the Aragon was the Vatican.

The daughter rolled her eyes again. I'm not sure if the mom noticed; if so, she ignored her, and went on to say the coolest thing in the entire universe.

"I saw a band play here called Jane's Addiction."

Part of my brain may have exploded.

She was in her forties, in a GAP logo sweatshirt with helmet hair. In my head, I'd slapped her with every possible generalization: *suburbs, tourist, old, out-of-touch, uncool,* everything I promised myself I would never become. Not once had I considered that there might be more to her story. That there is always more to our stories. She'd *been* there! She'd been *there,* ducking beer bottles and crowdsurfing while Perry climbed the walls. I wanted her to describe it, to put me there. I wanted to feel the music vibrate through my shoes.

But before I had a chance to ask, her daughter said, "Jane's Addiction? Who's that?"

I left before I flogged her.

11.

Upstairs in my condo, I went into the turret to look in on my napping son. Inside, it's not a perfect circle. More like a quarter-piece of pie; two flat walls meet at a right-angle connected by a ninety-degree curve. Our friend Kat, an artist, set up her ladders and painted a huge red tree, its leaves and branches twisting to the ceiling and reaching around the circumference of the room, a forest in the middle of the city. I fed my kid in that forest. I wrote there while he slept. I cried there while he cried, in the months following his birth when I lost myself in the fog, and it was there that I found myself, too; listening to him breath and talk and sing and laugh, the best fucking music in the world.

I put my hand on his sleeping back, feeling it rise and fall. Someday, he might look at me the way that woman's daughter looked at her, and that's okay. He might go to rock shows at the Aragon, ducking beer bottles and climbing the walls, and that's okay, too. He might read these essays, seeing how I tried and failed and tried again, and, hopefully, how there's always more to the story: mine and his and yours and yours and yours.

And on my grave—he'll know Jane's Addiction.

On my fucking grave.

12.

Later that night, I went out onto the balcony and looked across the street at the Aragon's enormous marquee, A-R-A-G-O-N running vertically top-to-bottom. Often, one or more of the electric neon letters are burnt out, spelling A-G-O-N or A-A-G-O or R-A-G-O-N. The club was dark that night, so the streets belonged to the city instead of a rock show. I was out there for a while, watching it; my front-row seat to so much messy beauty.

Then I got out my cellphone and called my son's godfather, my oldest friend, Jeff. "You have to promise," I said when he picked up. "Promise you'll tell him that once, I was cool."

Footnotes:

1. I've lived in Chicago for nearly two decades. Chicagoans have told me that that's long enough to call myself a Chicagoan. I think of myself as such, but in the interests of both full disclosure and hometown respect: hold up your right palm; I grew up about a half-inch west of the base of your thumb. Go Blue.
2. Why, Butthole Surfers? *Why?*
3. Unless we count musical theater, which in this case, I am not.
4. At that point in my life, I'd been to exactly two live concerts: 1) Lionel Richie's *Dancing on the Ceiling* tour with my mom—I remember the band suspended upside down on wires during the finale—and 2) an Indigo Girls show in Royal Oak. It was an outdoor amphitheater, and I was standing in a lovely patch of grass near some tiny, lovely trees—exactly where one should be when one is at an Indigo Girls concert. A very beautiful woman in a flowy skirt and a bikini top came up to me, said, "I love you, pretty girl," and hugged me. Then she went up to the tree I was standing next to, said, "I love you, pretty tree," and hugged it.
5. Apparently DTE Energy acquired the naming rights to Pine

Knob in 2002, and it's now called the DTE Energy Music Theatre. But fuck that noise. Pine Knob is Pine Knob. Comiskey Park is Comiskey Park. The Sears Tower is the Sears Tower. Now get off my lawn.

6. I don't know what happened to him. I don't remember how we began or how we ended, and it wasn't 'til writing this essay that I fully grasped what that concert meant to me. Thank you, sort-of boyfriend who took me to Lollapalooza. I am profoundly grateful.

7. I've lived and worked and hung out in many different neighborhoods in Chicago. The only time I ever feared for my immediate safety was in Wrigleyville when the bars closed. A guy chased me down the street, yelling that I should stop 'cause he just wanted to talk to me. Don't worry, he wasn't going to rape me or anything. Why wasn't I stopping? *Why wasn't I fucking stopping?*

8. Dear Katie and Steve: ♥

9. I'd also tell her: talk less, listen more.

10. Marilyn Manson owes me a tree.

FICTION

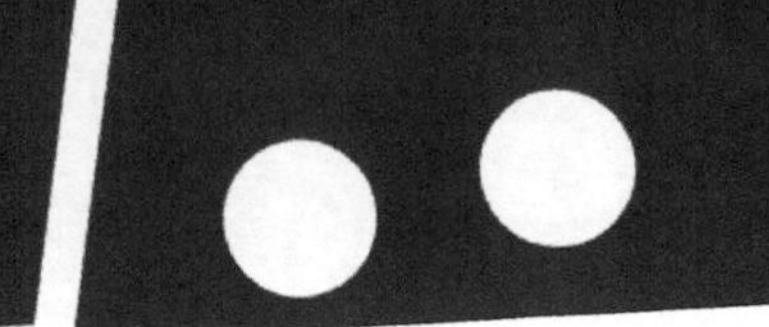

ANALOGUE

by Jay Hosking

ANALOGUE

THIS story begins right at this moment, with a twelve-inch plate of black vinyl between my hands and the bare shoulder of the most beautiful woman I have ever known in the periphery of my vision. The rest of the world has gone to bed and the only sound in her cluttered living room is the steady tapping of sleet against the window. Her breath is falling on the back of my t-shirt in tight bursts. The LP is almost close enough to kiss and it smells sharp and papery, like an old book. There is a picture of a familiar, thin, bearded man on the label at the centre of the record. I can still taste the metallic tang of blood in the back of my mouth.

She puts her hand on my elbow, gentle but unwavering, and I feel the muscles in my back relax.

"Go on," she says.

I curl my toes into the carpet and lift myself off the corner of her coffee table. In two steps I am at the record player, a direct-drive with a beautiful wood-grain plinth. I open the dust cover of the turntable with the ring finger and pinky of my right hand and carefully press the LP onto the platter. The *start* button is built into the plinth and exactly the size of my fingertip. When I press down on it, the drive spins to life and the tone arm lifts out of its cradle. The arm makes its way to the record but I catch it before the needle drops. As a rule, I don't like how automatics take the best parts away from you. So for a moment, to assert my control, I hold the tone arm in my hand and think about the concentric grooves on the LP spinning imperceptibly inwards, toward that wretchedly thin man near the woods.

And then with all my precision, I rest the stylus on the edge of the vinyl. I listen carefully to the sound that only a needle makes as it finds its path on a record, somewhere between the contemplation of a *hmm* and the definitive *thud* of an open hand against your front door. There is an instant where I turn and find her listening to that sound. Her hair is a mess of curls pushed behind her ears. A faint pattern of freckles is splashed across her nose and cheeks. I can see the delicate line of her collarbone as it passes under the strap of her dress and meets her shoulder. The bottom lids of her eyes are pushed upwards, making two sleepy crescents with green flecks inside. She looks at me like she is asking herself a question about me. All this passes in an instant. And then the music starts.

• • •

This morning, there was a dead body on the side of the Trans-Canada Highway. It was an hour of bumper-to-bumper traffic trying to cross a bridge into Vancouver. I kept my left foot on the brake pedal and my right foot on the gas all the way through. After three hundred thousand kilometres of road life and more than four thousand kilometres on this trip alone, Annie idles too low and I need to keep a steady injection of gasoline into the engine to prevent the old girl from stalling. I muttered to myself about the injustice of gridlock after four days of unfettered coasting down the highway, of being ground to a halt less than fifty kilometres from my destination.

Then I saw the dead motorcyclist on the side of the road, one foot and a bit of shin sticking out from under a blue tarp, and I stopped muttering. He was wearing a hiking boot and navy blue track pants with a white stripe down the side. The tarp was rustling in the wind and I imagined it repeatedly slapping against the dead man's helmet. The bike was pushed off to the very edge of the road's shoulder and looked as much like a motorcycle as meat looks like an animal. Just behind the bike was an SUV with a bent hood and broken headlight on the driver's side. And standing over it all was a thin man with a short beard, his bony jaw set tight and empty eyes fixed on the white-grey winter sky to the south.

Upon entering the city, I found some road parking for Annie and brought my things inside my new sublet. The sum of my remaining personal possessions included a cheap turntable with built-in pre-amp, a single milk crate of records, a pair of powered monitors with five-inch speakers, and a hockey bag half-filled with clothes. I scratched at the rust just above Annie's front wheel and thought about getting it repainted or repaired.

I spent what was left of the morning setting up the record player and speakers and then scrubbing away four days of driving under the hot water of the showerhead. I had no soap and no towel; I dried myself with a t-shirt from the hockey bag. To mark the occasion, the first record I played was *Shots* by Vancouver's Ladyhawk. I clipped my fingernails and sang along. And then I headed out again.

Coaxing the gas with one foot and the brakes with the other, I soon hit Main Street. The mountains were to the right, and a hill of storefronts was to the left. I turned left. Main Street didn't look much like a main street but it would probably have what I needed. It could never have been mistaken for Toronto, though, with its severe incline and irregularly spaced storefronts. I put Annie in a grocery store parking lot just off Main.

We are all sensitive to our vices but some of us are more sensitive than others. I could have gone to one of the coffee shops or even the corner store and asked them about where I could find a cell phone store. Instead, I saw a small swirl of neon in a window and a hand-painted sandwich board advertising vinyl just up the road. I told myself I could ask there about phones. Before I even reached the doorstep I knew what I would find: almost no jazz or R&B, a shitty used section full of '70s rock, but a great collection of small-label rock/pop and hip hop from the last few years. There was a sleigh bell hanging from the doorframe and it punctuated my entrance with one sharp *ring*.

Side A of Sonic Youth's *Rather Ripped* was playing over the store stereo, and I could see it spinning on a belt-driven table near the cash register. There were two voices coming from the back room and no one up front. I took my time. The stacks weren't too tight but there were some real gems, including Rachel Grimes' *Book of Leaves* and the white pressing of Pinback's *Blue Screen Life.* Both were out of print and very difficult to find, and both would gouge into the small savings I had brought with me. I pulled the records close to my chest and turned to the register.

The cashier was a young woman. You know the woman I'm talking about: sleepy-eyed, freckled, curly brown hair to her chin. Her nose was thin and her bottom lip was full and her neck was smooth and slender. Her eyes were so wide I could see white above the green of her iris and I guessed she had been watching me for some time. Still, the look was more surprise than fear, the face of someone who was about to laugh with relief. And at the thought, I couldn't help but smile at her. It was the first time I ever laid eyes on her.

"Good record," I said when I got to the counter, meaning *Rather Ripped.* Side B was almost finished. I put my records down but kept my eyes on her.

And then she laughed. She was trying to keep it to herself but it just bubbled out of her. This would have been the moment when any other cashier grabbed my items and rang them in. She just stood there and looked at me and grinned. I was happy to receive her full attention even if I had no idea what the hell was going on.

"I like how the whole band comes in off the first beat of Side A," I said. "No pomp, you know?"

"No pomp," she repeated. She was still smiling at me. "You don't recognize me, do you?"

"I'm sorry, no. But unless you're from Toronto, you may

have me mistaken for someone else. I just arrived today."

The sleigh bell jingled and her eyes darted away from me for a moment. When she looked back at me, she was all business and focused on the records rather than my face. One hand absentmindedly punched in the prices while the other tucked a curl behind her ear. The record ended and the needle began to drag along the edge of the centre label. She put my purchases in a paper bag and handed them to me. I wanted to keep the conversation going.

"Can I ask you a favour? Could you point me in the direction of the nearest cell phone store?"

"There's a place just down the street," she told me, shifting her eyes to the other customer in the shop. "You know what? I'll just walk you there."

I'm sure she could see the surprise in my face.

"It's a good time for me to get lunch, anyway," she explained and smiled.

She opened the back door, signalled to the other clerk, and grabbed a jean jacket from under the counter. We squeezed single-file between an aisle of records and the other customer, a thin man with his back to us. The air had gotten much colder outside and she pulled her jacket tight. She turned to me after we'd walked a few feet down the street and I realized that I was still smiling.

"I'm Annie," she said. "I'm sure you were just about to ask."

She put out her hand and I took it in mine. It was a good shake, the kind where the webs between your index fingers and thumbs touch. Her hand was narrow and strong and warm.

"Matt," I told her. "Hey, my car's name is Annie."

"Should I be flattered?" She grinned and started walking again.

"Sure. She's the most dependable woman I know."

"Of course you'd say that."

Main Street seemed a little more bustling now with people and dogs and traffic. Annie, the person, was wearing small brown sneakers without any laces. I looked up and she was squinting a little because her hair was whipping into her face. The image of the blue tarp thrashing against the dead motorcyclist came back to me.

"*Et voila*," she said and waved her arms. It took me a moment but then I realized we were in front of the cell phone store.

"Thanks so much."

She said slowly, "You know, we do know each other. Or at least I know you. And even if you like shitty records like *Rather Ripped*, I'm thankful for a nice conversation, too."

"Hang on a sec. *Rather Ripped* is shitty? That's blasphemy."

"The third song kills the momentum and the album never gets it back."

"OK, I can see how you might make that mistake," I said. "Seriously, though, where do you think we know each other from?"

"I'll tell you over dinner tonight. Shake on it and the deal is done."

Her smile was coy but not joking. I was missing some key piece of information that would justify the logic of her request and she knew it. Her sneakers were pointing in at each other a little and her arms were wrapped around her body for warmth. She cocked an eyebrow as if to say, *So?* Finally, I put my hand out for her to shake.

"I can live with that," I said, "and I'll probably enjoy it, but I won't pretend to understand it."

"Could be worse," she said and put her hand into mine, this time for a little longer.

She scribbled on an old receipt, put it in my hand, and then she turned on her heels and hurried down the road. I watched her a little and then looked the opposite direction on Main Street, back toward the record shop. The other customer was just leaving the store, his frail hands empty and his jaw framed by a dark beard. His eyes looked like two black dots.

• • •

Back at the sublet, I put on my new Rachel Grimes record and flopped onto the bed. The mattress was still bare and smelled foreign. I considered doing something about it but chose to lie there instead, reading Annie's invitation over and over. When evening crept in, I changed into the nicest clothes in my hockey bag. I looked almost presentable with my pea coat and a little water through my hair.

I took the car because I didn't want to be late and didn't

really know where I was going. I ended up being twenty minutes early and standing in the drizzling rain. By the time she got off the bus and wandered up to me, I was shivering a little.

"Hi, Annie," I said.

"Hello, Matt. Long time no see."

She had exchanged her sneakers for little black boots and her jean jacket for a grey tweed coat. Both boots and coat were too light for an Ontario winter but probably perfect for Vancouver. The skirt of a simple green dress was poking below the coat and she wore black tights with it. The jacket's hood was pulled over her curls. She looked cute.

"What happened to the above-zero winter?" I asked.

"Even Vancouver freezes sometimes," she said and took me by the hand to a Vietnamese restaurant. I couldn't look her in the eyes when she was touching me.

"I love Vietnamese," I told her. She nodded.

The place was small and decorated in mostly black and white. We took a seat by the window and only let go of each other's hands to take off our coats. Directly outside the restaurant, Commercial Drive was relatively quiet for my tastes but I liked the modest presentation of the storefronts. She ran the edge of her thumb along the back of my hand and my cheeks burned because of it.

"I made a deal with you," she said. "Would you like me to explain how we know each other?"

"Will it burst this bubble?"

"It might."

"Then let's wait a minute."

The waitress came with tea and went with our order. Annie smelled like lavender and the skin on her hand was soft. We sat in a very nice silence.

After a couple minutes, I let go of her hand and said, "OK We better burst it. This is starting to feel normal."

"I was hoping you'd remember something," she said. "I wanted you to have at least a glimmer of recognition."

She took a long pause and I took a sip of tea.

"We lived together for two years," she said.

She looked away and I scanned my memory for interpretations.

"What, were you one of the people who lived in the basement of the Markham place?"

"Not in Toronto," she said. "Here."

"Huh? I told you I just got to Vancouver, right? This is literally my first day here. And you're telling me we were roommates?"

"No. I'm telling you we *lived together*. Like in the way where we sleep in the same bed."

"For two years?"

"Yes."

I laughed dismissively and said, "Oh, OK."

"Don't be a prick," she snapped. The line under each eye was especially pronounced and she looked genuinely upset. "Just because you don't understand it doesn't mean it's not true."

I could feel regret curdle my stomach.

"OK," I said. "OK. This is important to you. I can see that. But you're right; I don't understand. Could you try explaining it to me?"

She cupped her hands around her tea and said, "Five years ago, you drove here from Toronto and ended up staying. We met at a record convention just up the street from here. You started coming into the store pretty regularly. I don't know when I started looking forward to your visits. It felt like it happened overnight. And then I let you take me to dinner. Here, actually. 'Our courtship', you always called it. A year after that we moved in together."

She was choking up and her neck was going flush.

She said, "It wasn't perfect but it was really nice, you know?"

"It sounds nice, yeah," I said, "but you realize that couldn't have been me, right? I've never even been to Vancouver before today. I don't want reality to get in the way of our reunion dinner but I can't see any other way around it."

There was a break in the conversation. She kept her eyes on the window and I kept mine on the table. Eventually the waitress brought our meals and our stalemate continued. I could rationalize my dissatisfied feeling to being attracted to her or to feeling so untethered from the life I'd driven away from, but part of me wanted there to be something else.

"OK," I said. "Humour me. Why did we break up, then? Why am I the amnesiac and not you?"

It wasn't like a dam bursting. Her head was still turned away from me and nothing about her face changed suddenly, but it was there. The muscles around her lips got tighter and tighter and her eyes started to fill up until only surface tension was keeping the tears from spilling over. And then they did, fast streaks down her smooth skin, and all the tears followed that path down her face and dripped off the line of her jaw. All this time she was motionless and the only indication that anything was happening was that tension in her face.

I didn't know what to do. My own eyes were filling up a little. I reached out and put my fingertips on her cupped hands as gently as I could.

"Hey," I said, "Hey, I'm sorry. Come back to me please."

"I know basically everything about you," she told me, turning her eyes but not her head. "Your car. I know you named your car after your aunt. It stalls all the time."

"How—" I began. She cut me off.

"The only thing you can keep neat and tidy are your fingernails. Your aunt gave you her record player and her old vinyl collection when you were a teenager, and you thought Jethro Tull was the coolest thing you had ever heard. You prefer turntables with built-in pre-amplification but you feel guilty about it because it's not the old-fashioned way. You sing along with everything but feel like you're a mediocre musician."

"What the hell is going on, here?" I asked. I pushed my bowl and chopsticks to the side of the table.

She sniffled and continued, "And you consider yourself a good driver because you've never had an accident, but you don't even understand the concept of turning in the same direction as a skid."

Her last comment caught me so off guard that I couldn't help but laugh a little. I said, "Seriously though, it *doesn't* make sense. If you're sliding to the left, why the hell would you turn to the left?"

"You could never admit that I might know better. You idiot. If you had just turned into the skid, you wouldn't have ended up under the wheels of a transport truck. I wouldn't have had to console *your* fucking family at *your* funeral or spend a year hating you for never listening to me."

I flagged the waitress and made the gesture for our bill.

"Annie, I'm sorry for your loss but I don't even know you. I don't know anything about you. I'm not denying how accurately you described me. But you're just a very pretty girl I met today. You are a stranger."

"No, I'm not," she said.

I settled the bill and we collected our things in silence.

• • •

Outside, the drizzle had turned into genuine drops that were so cold they stung when they hit my cheeks and hands. Just before a bus across the street pulled away, a thin man with a beard got on it. I would have sworn it was the same man from the record shop or from the motorcycle accident. Annie came out the door a few seconds later and looked exhausted. The two of us faced each other almost in defiance, and then she put her head on the lapel of my coat.

"Let me drive you home," I said. She dipped her head twice against my coat.

As I drove, she pointed the way through my foggy windshield. Commercial Drive got much less glamorous and few cars were sharing the road with us.

"Your favourite colour is green," I said.

"Blue. *Your* favourite colour is green." She was right.

"You're a cat person, not a dog person."

"No. We both prefer dogs."

"OK. Easy one. You were a humanities student, not science."

"Yes," she said.

"English literature."

"Graphic design. I went to college, not university."

"You're a neat freak."

"Only in the kitchen and bathroom. What's my favourite Blonde Redhead record?"

"*Melody of Certain Damaged Lemons.*"

"Not bad," she said and smiled.

We turned right and made a quick left into a dark residential neighbourhood. I pulled in behind an old van and left the car running, my right foot feeding the car a little gas. She was looking at the glove compartment and her curls were piled up on one another clumsily. I'm not sure why I did it but I reached out and put my fingers through her hair, gently scratching her scalp with my nails. She closed her eyes and focused on what I was doing.

I could feel her hair coiling and passing around my fingers. I killed the engine and listened to her steady breathing. There was something a little sharper about the sounds on the windshield and I guessed that bits of ice were starting to fall with the rain. Her hair felt nice in my hands but my nose was starting to run from the cold.

"Do you really think I'm that same person?" I asked.

"Yes."

"Can you understand why that's impossible for me to accept?"

"Yes."

"So where does that leave us?"

She looked over at me, calm at first and then a little wide-eyed. She gestured at the rear-view mirror with her head. I looked into it and saw a trickle of blood coming out of my right nostril.

"Shit," I said and wiped my nose with the back of my hand. In the car, the blood looked like a black streak across my knuckles.

She reached out and opened the car door while saying, "Come on."

I followed her down the sidewalk, onto a small stone path and up the stairs of a porch. I could feel something thick dripping down the back of my throat. She hurried me into the house and up two flights of stairs, unlocked another door, and led me around the corner to a bathroom. The blood was almost black, even in the bright light of her washroom. It took a lot of tissue and time before my nose dried up.

Padding down the hardwood floor of the hallway, I found

her sitting on one knee in a carpeted living room. The room was cluttered with books, records, stacks of papers, and leafy plants. There was a stereo system in the corner of the room and she had put on The Cardigans' *Gran Turismo*, a surprisingly commercial choice but a good one nonetheless. I didn't even know it had been pressed for vinyl. Her coat and sweater were folded over the edge of an old upholstered couch. When I stepped through the doorframe, she looked up and showed me the record she was holding. Her arms were slender and smooth.

"Sorry, I've never had a nosebleed like…"

I trailed off when I looked closer at the cover of the LP. There was Annie, the girl, and Annie, the car. And there was someone who looked *exactly* like me. The background of the photo was all evergreen trees and blue sky, and my imposter had his arm outstretched like he was holding the camera. Annie the car was even rusted just above the driver's side front wheel. There were no words on the cover.

"Shit," I said and sat on the edge of her coffee table. My chest felt tight.

"Tell me, Matt," she began, "Why did you decide to come to Vancouver now?"

She lifted herself up and touched my shoulder. Her face was calm and serious. Then she turned away and stopped the record player.

"You need to listen to me carefully and not be so stubborn," she said. "Five nights ago, a man came into my room in the middle of the night and talked to me. I was terrified and thought I was dreaming until you arrived today. He told me you would be coming to Vancouver, again. He warned me not to get used to it, that he probably wouldn't let you stay long."

She sat down on the adjacent corner of the coffee table but I did not turn to look at her. I could only see her shoulder in the edge of my vision.

"Are you listening to me?" she asked. "You're a goof but you were always loyal to me. You won me by degrees. That record was our third anniversary present to each other. Take the record out."

I did as she said. On the label in the centre of the record was a photo of a gaunt man with a dark beard. His eyes were expressionless. I brought the record close to me to be sure.

"I recognize this man," I told her.

"He is the one who visited me five nights ago. I don't know where you got this photo from and you wouldn't tell me. I had never seen him until the other night. Now I know it's *impossible* for you to believe me but at least listen. He is a threat to you. He is a threat to us. I am not going through this again. If you can't take care of yourself then I will."

"But—"

"Oh Christ," she interrupted. "Really, Matt? You just have to fight this all the way, don't you? Put on the record."

• • •

And now the music starts. The chords are loosely played on a thin acoustic guitar. Behind the acoustic is a simple bass and drum rhythm that keeps a steady tempo and emphasizes beats two and four. And in the back of the mix is the sound of someone rapping their knuckles on the body of an electric guitar, leaving just the resonance of the strings and a hollow pit of reverb. I can hear the soft crackle of the vinyl as it regularly passes a small scratch on the disc.

A few bars in, a voice starts. I am not sure how long I listen but I know I have missed the words and am only listening to the timbre of my own voice. I have heard my recorded voice and found it alien; now, I hear a song I never recorded and know it is sung by me. The electric guitar sparks to life and the rhythm section follows. The song is building to something. I listen to the words.

I know you're asking why I did this

But he made for me a life.

I know you're asking why I'm leaving

But these choices have a price.

This entire time I have been staring past her into empty space but now my vision comes back and she is standing in front of me. The sight of her tugs at some familiar place in my abdomen. The space between us is disappearing even as my own voice continues over the speakers. The muscles near her nose tighten and her mouth opens a little, not a smile but something peaceful. We come closer still and our noses touch just before we kiss. There is just a little movement, the softness of our bottom lips pushing against each other and opening a little. It is a feeling I know intimately but I do not know how or why I could know it.

We lie on the bed in our clothes. Her head rests in the fold between my arm and chest. Our legs are folded and tangled together. She cries a little and it dampens my t-shirt. I cry a little, too. My free hand is in her hair again, rustling it, kneading and relaxing. I have nothing to say so I stay quiet. As she gets sleepy, she rolls away from me and I pull myself close behind her. And then I rest.

• • •

I know something is wrong when I awake. My eyes open slowly and I see the intruder standing in the doorway of the bedroom. I feel a pit in my stomach clench tight and hard and my shoulders pull toward my ears. The man is thinner than I remember and his dark clothes hang off him. His beard and eyes are the same colour as his jacket and his face looks like a white mask.

He slowly puts one finger up to his lips. *Shhh.* Then he rotates his arm a little and curls his finger toward himself twice. *Come here.* When I don't immediately obey, his head turns toward Annie and then back to me. I can sense that this little movement is both a threat and an offering of amnesty for the woman sleeping next to me. I get up and follow him down the stairs and out of the house. Chips of ice are still coming down with the rain. He glides to my car and opens the passenger door as if it hadn't been locked just a couple hours ago. I walk around to the driver's side and get in.

"Drive away," he says aloud. It is like hearing a voice through a cheap stereo, flat and distant. The only part of his face that moves is around his mouth. I start Annie and drive out of the parking spot. His bony hand reaches up and tilts the rear-view mirror so that we are looking at each other eye-to-eye even as I drive. It is inhuman how inert his face is.

My mouth is dry but I manage to ask, "Who are you?"

"That may be conceptually difficult for you," he says. He waves his left hand in a semicircle and continues lifelessly, "Imagine *all of this* were one of your records. A record collection is essentially a number of two-dimensional planes stacked beside each other. How would you explain to someone living on a record what you, a three-dimensional record collector, are? How do you explain depth, the concept of *in* and *out*, to someone who can only move up, down, left, or right? Turn right here and then take your next right."

I nearly stall Annie as I take her around the corner. Both my hands are tightly gripped on the wheel.

"What do you want, then?" I ask. I wipe my nose and find it is bleeding again.

"I am a collector," he says. "I want satisfying pieces for my collection. Take the off-ramp to your right. Imagine you cut two of your records and tried to paste the halves together. It would be hard to find two records whose halves could be pasted together and still make congruent sense, but let us say that I have a very large number of similar records. Do you follow?"

"No," I say. I exit as he instructed me and find myself on the Trans-Canada Highway, leaving the city the same way I entered it.

"I can make one great record from the lesser components.

The only limitation to the quality is my tools. In this case, there are some edges that need to be mended to make the conglomeration seamless."

"So I'm an edge to be mended?" I ask.

"In a sense," he responds and goes motionless again for a moment. "You were also an opportunity. The edges... they have never involved people before. We were curious to see if the overlap would have any residual effects."

"Who's *we*?"

My question goes unanswered. I stare at the husk beside me, not in the mirror but at him directly. His skin looks cold like a fish and he is deathly still. Outside of the car, the highway is mostly empty but brightly lit for overnight construction. We merge into the single lane of traffic, oncoming cars just on the other side of the reflective orange tube barriers. I wipe my nose again.

"Well, what did you find?" I ask him.

"You know as well as I do. We found you driving to Vancouver, drawn to a record store you didn't even know was there, and in bed with a stranger."

"She's not a stranger," I tell him. "So why are you even telling me this? Why are we here, on the highway?"

The rest of him does not move but his head turns to me and puts his gaze directly on me. I glance over to him, that sick feeling returning, and his eyes are black and flat like vinyl. He opens his mouth and bares his teeth and I wonder if he is trying to smile at me.

“I suppose I am fond of symmetry, and of fairness,” he says.

It all happens quickly. Without any warning or continuity, the passenger seat beside me is now empty and unused. I can feel Annie lurch and stutter on the pavement. And some dim realization dawns on me.

I look up and squint at the bright lights rushing toward me. I feel the wheels spinning without friction on a patch of black ice. Annie’s back end is swinging to the left, cutting through the flimsy barriers and into oncoming traffic. I strangle the steering wheel and push my teeth hard into each other. My front tires are still parallel to the back ones and still, incredibly, I’ve got my right foot on the gas to keep Annie from stalling. The entire windshield is a glare, now. I think of my time in Vancouver, one day compressed into an instant of thought. I think of waking up beside Annie. And then it just happens. I keep my grip on the wheel and pull it hard to the left.

I DON'T THINK SO

by Christopher Evans

I DON'T THINK SO

WE got high and followed people in Marnie's old Plymouth. It was 1991. Her big sister let her have the car when it was too embarrassing to drive anymore. The rear seat was slung so low you needed a hand to get out, and the fabric that lined the roof back there had peeled off so it bubbled down like a veil in an opium den. The car we were tailing was some kind of sedan.

The sedan was grey or maybe blue. I couldn't tell because I was wearing my sunglasses with the red lenses. The lenses turned all the blues and greens and greys into charred bloodclots and the whites and pinks and yellows into electric magma. The blacks stayed black. It was summertime, hot and cruel.

The sedan was driven by an older couple—button-down suburbanites—which enraged Marnie, who I hadn't slept with yet, and might never. Marnie hated the establishment and all their trappings—cardigans, dental care, expensive cheeses. She thought that anyone who had it better than she did should fuck off and die. Actually die.

We followed the couple out of the parking lot at Town & Country Mall and up the Old Island Highway, away from the city. Marnie plugged in her Sonic Youth *Goo* cassette and when the intro to "Kool Thing" came on she cranked up the stereo—the already half-blown speakers translating the music into trebly shards of raw noise—and gunned it, so we were right alongside them. As we smoked our cigarettes and stared them down, the woman rolled up her window—panicky, stricken—and mouthed either "What do you want?" or "One to two wands?" Marnie and I just laughed and drifted back behind them.

This continued through the outskirts, past the car dealerships and the mini-golf, and further from town, up the mountain. The man in the driver's seat kept turning around and looking behind at us. Eventually Marnie started to do the same—look back—and, after a while, turned Sonic Youth down and said, "I think we're being followed." While she was distracted, the sedan faded off into the parking lot of a Bino's Family Restaurant, the driver's eyes a flash of relief in the mirror.

I looked in the sideview in time to see another crimson landboat—another Chrysler—looming on my side, some tinny squall from the Chrysler's stereo cutting through the wind that screamed through our open windows. There was a girl in the driver's seat and a boy riding shotgun—in sunglasses, like us. Their cigarettes hung slack, ashes jetting behind them to pile in the back seat. I leaned out the window and shouted, "One to two wands!" They laughed and their car dropped behind ours.

Marnie smacked the dashboard and said, "Those callous fucks." Sometimes, Marnie was the wrong kind of too much.

At the stoplight by the abandoned water slides, they pulled up next to us and the driver, the girl, said, "You're in the wrong car." She was right. I got out, left my door hanging open, and crawled across her lap to sit between the two of them. Marnie swore bloody revenge and turned off, the passenger door slamming back into the frame. We continued up the highway.

They were siblings, and blonde. I didn't know their music, some kind of European brutalism with horns. I asked the girl if we could start dating now, but she just smirked and threw her cigarette out the window into the dry grass. I asked if I could kiss her and she said, "No." Her brother said I could kiss him and I did, but didn't like it. We drove through sleepy shitkicker towns until the angry lava sky began to darken, our lungs swollen with acrid haze.

A maroon shape scuttled into the road and the girl, the driver, swerved to hit it. It thumped and winged past—inert eyes, spattered teeth. I asked if I could take off my sunglasses and lie down for a bit, but the brother said, "No." He lit another cigarette with something oily inside. The girl kept checking her rearview and said, "I think we're being followed." Headlights backlit the cabin. Our faces were red, red, red.

At the stoplight by the burnt-out motel, a sedan pulled alongside us, blue or maybe green, radio cranked to a moderate volume—AM Gold. My parents.

My mother leaned out the window. "You're in the wrong car." I got out over the brother's lap and tried to climb in between my mother and father. My father hiked his thumb behind him. "Back seat, Squirt."

The Chrysler peeled off to the left, birds flipped through the windows, and we kept going, up the highway, up the mountain. My father reached back, yanked the sunglasses from my face, and sent them spiralling into the night. "Do up your belt." My mother handed back an afghan she'd been knitting—needles still tucked in her hair—and a glass of tepid milk. Amid the blackness, under roof fabric that didn't sag, I lay down across the seat to a lullaby of buttercream vocals and airbrushed guitar, and slept a sleep like my eighteen years had never even happened, or ever would again.

MY LOLITA EXPERIMENT

by Leesa Cross-Smith

MY LOLITA EXPERIMENT

SINCE *words without experience are meaningless*, I'd been giving purposeful meaning to all of the books I'd read and reread lately. Went fishing after *The Old Man and The Sea.* Set two of my friends up after finishing *Emma.* Took my English class to the courtroom to visit a trial-in-progress after we read *To Kill A Mockingbird.* I stole a lip gloss after I read *Crime and Punishment*, bought a witchy-black dress after *Harry Potter* and a bow and arrow after *Hunger Games.* I threw a chandelier and champagne dinner party for *The Great Gatsby* and planted my first tomatoes after *A Secret Garden.* I got some soft rabbits from the pet store after teaching *Of Mice and Men*, went jewelry shopping after *Lord of the Rings.*

Nathan Waller was my *Lolita* experiment. He was a freshman in college and I still taught at the high school, but the fact that he was one of my students just a year before worked for me. It wasn't like I could get in trouble for anything. He was smart and eighteen.

We'd driven eighty miles to a jankety outlet mall. The air was apple juice—some kind of smell the candle shop was piping out. It'd rained all night and morning. My hair felt wet but wasn't; I kept checking to make sure. Nate's dishy drummer-hair was wavy, flipping out over his shoulders like duck feathers. The apple juice smell made me thirsty. We stopped in the coffee shop for drinks. I whispered *my little cup brims with tiddles* into Nate's ear after the barista handed me my tall soy pumpkin spice latte.

Nathan, light of my life, fire of my loins. My sin, my soul. Nathan. Na. Than. He was Nate, plain Nate, in the morning, standing six feet one in two grey and orange sneakers. He was Nate-dog, the Nate-anator, a long-haired sometimes-Bro in a hooded college sweatshirt.

I made him a mix called *this love is good* and filled it with all kinds of songs about gooey-love, real and true. "This Love" by Taylor Swift. "I Second That Emotion" by Smokey Robinson & The Miracles. "At Last" by Etta James, "Love is Strange" by Mickey & Sylvia, "The Light" by Common. Debbie Gibson, Phil Collins, Fleetwood Mac, Joni Mitchell, Lauryn Hill.

I made him a mix called *you've earned it* and filled it with all kinds of songs about sex and sweaty-sticky-passion. "Earned It" by The Weeknd. "Two Weeks" by FKA Twigs. "Sex on Fire" by Kings of Leon. "Purple Rain" by Prince. "Wicked Game" by Chris Isaak. Portishead. The xx, Tricky, The 1975, Ellie Goulding, Frank Ocean, Sublime, D'Angelo, The Black Keys.

I made him a mix called *don't touch me; i'll die if you touch me* and filled it with all kinds of songs about love-doom. "Born to Die" by Lana Del Rey. "Babe I'm Gonna Leave You" by Led Zeppelin. "Skeleton Key" by Margot & the Nuclear So and So's (twice, once at the beginning and once at the end). Dashboard Confessional, Weezer, Billie Holiday, Belle and Sebastian, Joy Division.

He was the drummer in a popular local band so I was always trying to impress him with my music references. Sometimes I would write *love, love will tear us apart again* on my arm with a thin black Sharpie. When we got into an argument I'd pull up the sleeve of my cardigan sweater so he could see it.

When I told him I was ending it I touched his face and said perhaps, somewhere, some day, at a less miserable time, we may see each other again. He said he wasn't miserable. I said Me Neither. I handed him my copy of *Lolita*, dog-eared and underlined, hoping he would be able to read it like a map—find his way to someone else or back to me.

I was forcing tragedy although I liked him a lot. He was funny and had great arms, a soccer player's ass. *I am not, and never was, and never could have been, a brutal scoundrel,* so I let him keep a pair of my panties. I let him keep his key to my place, praying he'd use it.

IF THEY HAD MUSIC

by Will Johnson

IF THEY HAD MUSIC

KATE lets the seawater lick her toes. Waves slap against the hull of the sailboat as it sways in the afternoon breeze. The sails flap against the mast far above her head. She takes a slug of red wine and looks out at the arbutus trees that line the nearby beach, their bark peeling off in long, curled strips that expose the milky yellow wood underneath.

"You know that used to be a leper colony," Sebastien says, in that pretentious voice Kate hates. He plucks at a small banjo in his lap.

She has already heard this story. She knows she's looking at D'Arcy Island, that the lepers were primarily Chinese immigrants, and that this all happened less than a century ago. She knows this because Sebastien told her the last time they came here, but he always repeats himself when he's stoned.

"I wonder if they had music," she says.

"What?"

"Music. I mean they're out here all isolated with no family, no government or anything. I just wonder if they had music."

"You're missing the point," Sebastien says.

Kate doesn't want to fight. She wants to enjoy the sun on her shoulders, the music drifting up from below deck and the pleasant rhythms of the ocean surging underneath them.

"What's the point, then?" she asks. "Why don't you go ahead and tell me what the point is, Sebastien?"

She might be a little drunk.

"I'm talking about human suffering here."

She's had to pee for a while, so now seems like a good time. She rises to her feet and braces herself against the mast. Across the water she can see Cadboro Bay, the marina and the seaside mansions that lead up the hill to the University of Victoria. Between her and the beach the ocean swirls and crashes and roils up into frothy white waves. The wind is picking up.

"Should we head back?" she asks.

"Soon," says Sebastien. "I wanted to go for a swim, maybe."

"It's starting to look rough."

Sebastien ignores her. She makes her way back along the deck, stepping carefully in her bare feet. She rests her half-full bottle of wine beside the motor, shimmies out of her underwear, hikes up her dress and crouches over the railing. She watches Sebastien rise up and sink down in front of her. His long blond hair flutters around his head and brushes against his pink, freckled shoulders. Sometimes she forgets how young he can look. She knows that sooner or later she's going to have to break up with him. But not today.

The boat bucks unexpectedly. Before Kate can react her legs are above her head, her ankles tangled in her underwear. There's a brief second where she can see everything upside down, the sun-glinted waves posing as stormy sky. The island is like a cloud with arbutus trees hanging down into an empty blue void. Her face glances off the engine as she falls, then she feels the water close its arms around her and for a moment everything is silent. She breaks the surface with a gasp and takes in a lungful of sea air. Her body has been jolted awake. Her eyes furiously try to blink away the streams of water running down her face.

"Kate, you okay?" Sebastien yells. "Kate?"

She waits for a moment, buffeted by the waves, to answer him. She listens to the wind and feels her body being carried, weightless, away from the boat.

• • •

Kate moved to Victoria from Hamilton the year she graduated from high school. She wanted to live beside the ocean and she wanted to go to university far away from her parents. The first time she walked down to Cadboro Bay and took off her shoes, she let her toes sink into the sand and knew she had made the right decision. She loved the saltwater smell in the air.

She met Cliff at a bluegrass concert downtown about two months after she started school. He was playing stand-up bass and she liked the way he closed his eyes while he fingered the strings, the way he stomped his foot and smiled as he rocked his head back and forth to the music. She brought him back to her residence building and let him take her in the communal showers. Afterwards he sat on her bed and played the guitar. She rested her feet in his lap.

Cliff introduced her to mushrooms during a weekend trip to his cabin on Gabriola Island. The experience floated by her like a dream. Late at night they sat together at the top of some jagged rocks and watched the waves slosh through the barnacles. She loved the violent roar of the purple water, the way the mist drifted up and tickled her face. She felt like she understood everything.

Cliff invited her on tour with him during reading break. His band was called The Saltwater Sultans, and they traveled up the Malahat Highway in an old bus. They played their instruments the entire way, passing a joint back and forth and taking deep swigs from a bottle of Jamieson's. There were three other girls on the trip, but Kate barely noticed them. Instead she noticed Shane, the lead singer. Shane had effortlessly messy shoulder-length brown hair and ocean-blue eyes. His voice was a plaintive wail, as most of their songs were about being down and out, poor and lonely. Cliff noticed the way she looked at his friend and later in the parking lot of their venue he screamed at her and grabbed her by the arm. "You can't fucking treat people like this," he said.

That night, while Cliff was passed out in his motel room, Kate fucked Shane on the floor of the bus. They smoked pot and laid naked together in a pile of ratty old blankets that were covered in oil stains. Kate played with the curly hair of his beard and listened to him talk. She watched him lick his lips, watched his tongue flick inside the cavern of his mouth, watched him form his words and breathe them out like a song.

• • •

Kate mops the surface of a small table with a wet rag. She picks up a few empty glasses, foam still bubbling in the bottom, and balances them on her tray as she sweeps back towards the bar. Above her countless bras dangle from the ceiling, stapled at random amidst flyers, stickers and crumpled pornographic playing cards. Kate shoulders her way through a crowd of students and makes her way past the regulars, who sit slumped on their bar stools and stare blankly at the dark ceiling. It's not too busy tonight. She maneuvers around the counter and slides her tray down. She taps her foot to the Johnny Cash tune blaring from the speakers mounted in the rafters.

"Table four's looking a little low," the bartender mutters. He fills a pint glass with a foamy, dark-brown lager and doesn't bother to look up.

"On it," she says.

Kate loves Big Bad John's. She likes the intimacy of the tiny space, the feel of peanuts crackling under her cowboy boots, the familiar faces in the shadowy corners. When she's not working she sits with the elderly regulars and listens while they push drinks in her direction. She's intrigued by the wrinkles around their eyes, by their raspy voices and their meandering stories. She asks about their families, about their wives at home. She swings by table four and asks if they want refills, but they wave her off. She's about to sneak outside for a smoke break when Shane walks in the front door and starts searching above the crowd. His cheeks are sunburned and he's wearing crooked sunglasses with black electrical tape around one arm.

"You think you can just walk in here?" she says.

Shane cocks his head to one side and grins. He opens his arms and she slinks into them with a smile, nuzzling up to his stubbly neck. They hug for a long moment, and Kate smells his overwhelming musk—a mixture of campfire and body odor, and maybe the slightest hint of marijuana.

"What'd you do to your eye?" he asks. He leans back to gently touch the half-healed wound. "That looks like a nasty one."

"Three stitches. Fell off a fucking sailboat," she says.

"Of course you did," he says. He rustles her hair.

After work she comes outside to find Shane kicking angrily at a lock attached to his bike wheel. He curses under his breath while a cigarette dangles from between his lips. She looks at his filthy denim jacket, his bright red plaid sweater and his filthy jeans.

"Sorry, I keep forgetting the code," he says. He fumbles with the lock for a few more moments until it finally releases.

As they bike through the empty streets, Shane hums quietly into her ear. Kate can tell he's been drinking all day. She sits perched on his handlebars, her hands over top of his. She can feel his chest against her back. Her feet dangle over the pavement that whips by underneath them. Tears from the wind tremble in the edges of Kate's eyes. They descend into James Bay and head towards her house, randomly wobbling on and off the sidewalk. The handlebars dig into the backs of her legs, but she still feels like she's floating. It's been over nine months since Shane went away.

"How was Nicaragua?" she asks.

• • •

The Saltwater Sultans broke up after Shane and Kate got together. He started played solo gigs at restaurants and Kate would attend each one. She usually got some free food and she relished the sidelong glances she got from the stage. Afterwards she would get shit-faced with Shane and stumble into his tiny apartment half undressed. She got a job teaching swimming lessons in her second year. She was only taking three classes, so she spent most of her time at the swimming pool or at Shane's gigs. Though she slept at his house most nights, he didn't like the idea of having her move in. So she kept her small apartment, which was usually empty, cold and full of dirty dishes. She only cleaned up when her parents flew out to visit.

She met Neil during a late night shift on a Monday night. The pool was mostly deserted and they stood on deck gossiping about the other lifeguards. He seemed awkward and a little nervous around her, but she liked the way he tapped his fingers on his leg while he nodded along to the music. Sure enough, it turned out he was a drummer. A month later Shane's percussionist quit and Kate suggested Neil as a replacement. Neil didn't have much of a background in bluegrass but he could keep a beat. Shane and Neil had a quick chemistry, and pretty soon they were playing every gig together. Kate watched her two friends and felt like she was building a family. She liked being part of their trio.

Then one day Shane asked Kate to perform with them. He needed female vocals on a few songs and they spent a week practicing. She bought a cute white dress and a new pair of boots, and during the songs she wasn't needed she just danced beside him. She loved the way her hair swept across her shoulders, how it flew into her face and tossed up into the air in time with the music. She could feel Neil's eyes on her as she bounced. His timing was flawless and she let his beats carry her back and forth across the stage. Shane looked at her like she was a magical creature, his eyes full of affection. She felt like a gypsy.

They toured the Gulf Islands and up to Nanaimo, playing gigs at bars and restaurants. They named themselves The Islanders. One night they played on a beach, with the moon glinting off the water. Shane strummed his guitar and Neil banged on a drum between his knees, both of them perched on a piece of driftwood, while she danced in the sand. She liked the cold air on her bare legs.

But then Shane announced that he was going traveling. He felt cloistered and stifled in Canada, and he needed to move on. At first Kate wanted to ask if she could come with him to South America, but then she thought of her parents in Ontario and how disappointed they would be. She only had two more years left of her Psychology degree. Neil drove them both to the airport and Kate cried as she watched Shane disappear down the ramp.

Neil held her and she liked the way his hands felt strong on her lower back. That night they got stoned and had a bath together. She traced her fingers along his moist skin and felt his eyes on her naked body. They had awkward sex on the linoleum of her kitchen floor.

Over the next few weeks she watched Neil change. When he drummed his fingers against the steering wheel it had a heavier staccato. But without Shane around, Neil stopped playing gigs. Sometimes Kate would come over to his house to find out he hadn't slept for two days. She found empty pill bottles in his jacket pockets, wadded up balls of aluminum foil were scattered around his apartment, and there was powder crusted around the edge of his credit card. One day she found him on the floor of his bathroom foaming at the mouth. When the paramedics arrived they loaded him on to a stretcher and rolled him out into the street. They wouldn't let her in the ambulance. The flashing lights disappeared around a corner.

• • •

Kate watches Sebastien pace across his living room. He is clenching and unclenching his fist and periodically punching it against his thigh. She wonders what would happen if she stood up and walked out of his house. She could call a cab and never talk to him again. But instead, she sits and waits for him to say something.

"This is so predictable," he says. "I mean, of course."

His voice catches in his throat.

Kate can feel tears oozing down her cheeks but she figures it's from stress more than anything else. She has known all along that when Shane returned from Nicaragua she was going to end things with Sebastien. But she's never been any good with conflict. Her feelings never get properly expressed in words and most of the guys she'd been with over the years could out-talk her in every situation. She stares at the carpet.

"I don't want this anymore," she says.

"Sorry?" says Sebastien. "Sorry? I couldn't hear you, Kate. Sorry?"

"I should go."

Before she realizes what is happening, Sebastien has grabbed her by the arms and slammed her against the wall. She whimpers. She can feel his hot breath on her face. His fingers pinch into the skin of her arms. She opens her mouth to scream but he forces the meat of his palm into her open mouth. Her head bounces off the drywall and she feels dizzy.

"I fucking love you, do you hear me?" he says.

She should have brought Shane with her.

"How could you do this?"

"I'm sorry," she murmurs through his hand.

Kate can't figure out another way to handle the situation, so she grabs the waist of Sebastien's jeans and flips open the button. He blinks at her, surprised, his chest still heaving. She can see his face trembling and she knows how much she's hurt him. She undoes his zipper.

"You're sorry?" he says. "That's what you're saying?"

She slips her hand inside his boxer shorts and closes her eyes. He moans a little, releases his hand from her face, then thrusts against her. She closes her eyes and sinks to her knees. She feels his fingers clasp behind her head. She feels trapped and considers sprinting for the door. But she takes him in her mouth instead.

Sebastien fucks her on the living room couch, and she keeps her eyes closed the entire time. She wonders if he'll let her leave afterwards. She feels uncomfortable and he's hurting her, but she closes her eyes and tries to hear musical notes. She fixates on the rhythm of his hips and pretends it's the steady beat of a drum. When he finishes, he leans into her ear and whispers, "There's something wrong with you. Something missing."

• • •

Kate spent three days in the hospital while Neil was recovering from his overdose. She slept with her coat over her head on the uncomfortable waiting room benches. She nervously walked laps around the corridors and repeatedly went outside to chain-smoke cigarettes. Neil's roommate Tyler was listed as his emergency contact and he relayed most of the information to Kate. He couldn't take time off work, so he just made appearances in the morning and the evening. One night, before he headed home, he touched her face.

"This isn't your fault," he said. "You were good for him."

On the third day she met Neil's parents, the Solomons. His mother was tiny and didn't look much older than Kate.

She hardly spoke and stood slightly behind her husband. Neil's stepdad introduced himself as Scott, and squeezed Kate's hand a little too hard. While they were talking, he repeatedly checked his cell phone.

Scott informed her that Neil was being transferred to a psychiatric unit on the Mainland. He told her it probably wasn't a good idea for her to visit. He shook his head apologetically and Neil's mother began to cry. Scott ushered her away, and Kate never saw any of the Solomons again. She walked out of the hospital, went straight home and slept for nearly twenty hours. She spent the following weeks in a constant state of inebriation and nearly failed her classes. One night she got into an argument with a bartender and was about to be thrown out by the bouncer when Sebastien stepped in. He dropped a twenty-dollar bill on the bar and explained that Kate was his sister. She was too confused and drunk to interfere and she let this total stranger lead her out on to the street by the shoulders.

Kate woke up the next morning while he was having a shower. She saw a banjo leaning against the dresser and decided it was a sign. He was unemployed and a year younger than her, but she liked knowing she wouldn't have to sleep alone. She went to some of his gigs, which were underwhelming, but then one day he took her down to Cadboro Bay and showed her his parent's sailboat. It was small, and they had fallen behind on the maintenance. But as soon as she stepped onboard and felt the way the deck shifted under her feet she knew she could be Sebastien's girlfriend.

• • •

Kate rides the bus into James Bay and looks out the window at the marina. Tourists are listening to buskers and taking pictures as hundreds of sailboats rock in the afternoon breeze. She watches the seagulls flap their wings lazily as they soar far above their heads. She wants to find Shane, get stoned and disappear for a while.

When she gets to Shane's house, a bored-looking teenage girl answers the door and tells her he isn't home. Kate walks around to the backyard and finds his bike chained up where they left it. She remembers the code from the other night and she takes it. She pedals calmly through the suburban streets, up and down hills, as if she's in a trance. She doesn't realize she knows where she's going until she coasts down the hill past the university and bikes into the park near Cadboro Bay. She chains it up and follows the beach to the small rowboat that Sebastien keeps tethered to a tree. She drags it down to the shore, throws her purse and her shoes into it, then jumps in and starts yanking on the oars. When she reaches his sailboat, which is moored half a kilometer out, she fastens the rowboat to the side and climbs in. She knows where he keeps the keys to the motor. Within a few moments she's slicing towards D'Arcy Island.

While the waves crash against the hull and Kate squints into the sun, she thinks about the last three years. She thinks about all the people who have come and gone, and wonders if she has any real friends. She feels like an outcast. She wishes she felt something like guilt for the way she treated the men in her life, but she feels numb. She thinks about the words Sebastien said to her, his breath hot against her ear. *There's something wrong with you.* She shudders while she steers. *Something missing.*

She anchors near the island and sits quietly for a while, looking at the waves and the trees. She thinks about the lepers who lived out the end of their lives here. She wonders where they were buried. Then she goes below deck and retrieves a bottle of red wine and Sebastien's banjo. She has to stop herself from hurling it in the water. She's decided she'll row back and leave the sailboat out here, a few kilometers from shore, just to fuck with him. In the meantime, she sits with her feet hanging into the water and starts to pluck at the banjo. At first she's clumsy and the strings hurt her fingers. But then she finds a pick and starts to figure it out. She murmurs under her breath for a while and then she starts to sing. She opens up to the wind and her voice is carried away.

INVISIBLE STRINGS

by Steve Karas

AKI is lying on the stage, shredding away at his air guitar to "And Justice for All," his shoulder blades against the hardwood holding up his torso, his pelvis thrusting. His eyes are shut tight and he's lost in the solo like he's on his bedroom floor and not in front of hundreds of people at 45 Special, a legendary Finnish rock bar. He jumps up and bangs his head, stomps around the stage, cranks out the next riff, the air guitar behind his head, the air guitar between his legs in horse-riding position, the air guitar vertical in a twelve o'clock pose. He finishes with a windmill, and the crowd, Penelope in the front row, whistles and applauds. The stage lights heat his face, sweat drips from his long snarl of hair. He sticks out his tongue, raises the metal horns, and prays his performance will be enough to get him through to the next round.

• • •

Aki and Penelope, wearing matching black T-shirts, hold hands and amble through the hotel lobby. The complimentary "Air Guitar World Championships" bag is strewn across Aki's back. The concierge is the opposite of him—tall, pale-skinned, neatly cut mouse-brown hair. He smiles as he checks in guests, but Aki senses he's watching them, judging them. They already asked him how much a room would cost and know they can't afford one. Still, they hang around the front desk like stray cats circling dinner tables for scraps. Beyond getting to Finland, they hadn't thought through much else.

Aki's cell phone vibrates in his skinny jeans. It's a text from his brother. *Pou 'se, malaka?* it reads. *Where are you, jagoff?* Aki slides it back into his pocket.

They sit in the shiny leather lobby chairs and spread the map open between them. Penelope's black hair dangles over the Gulf of Bothnia. Aki yawns; he hasn't gotten much sleep of late. She points to a hostel in the village of Kello, about 25 kilometers north of Oulu. "Let's see if there's a bus that goes to it," she says.

The American steps out of the lift. He resembles an Orthodox priest—hair pulled back into a ponytail, long beard draping from his face—but for the red Spandex, the white-framed sunglasses, the AC/DC cutoff. "Nice job, Air-istotle. You riffed our faces off."

Aki nods sheepishly, says thank you. The American is last year's champion. He was interviewed on the BBC and does Dr. Pepper commercials now on American television. "Air

Jesus" they call him. He slurps from a can of Sandels Finnish beer. There are contestants from twenty different countries, and each has a nickname. Aki—the Greek—goes by "Air-istotle." There's the Belgian, Hans "Van Dammage" Van Deer Meer and the Argentinian, Santiago "Buenos Air-ace" Carrizo. Hirotaka "Electric Ninja" Kinugasa is representing Japan.

At sixteen, Aki is the youngest competitor here. Five months back he had never even heard of the competition. The drummer in his old band signed him up for the Greek nationals at the last minute, and, somehow, he won. He's been practicing every day since. Penelope is the only person who sees his routines before he goes on stage.

"What are you guys looking for?" the American asks, his beard rippling as he speaks.

"The hostel," Penelope says. "Do you know it?"

"That's far, dudes. You need a place to crash? Crash in my room. It has two beds."

Another competitor, this one in a Viking costume, marches through and bumps his beer against Air Jesus's. "*Kippis*, motherfucker!"

"Let's go party," Air Jesus says.

Aki and Penelope's eyes meet. She nods in agreement, so he folds up the map and stuffs it into the bag as his cell phone buzzes again. He barely pulls it from his pocket, hesitates to look at the message. *Malaka! Pou sto dialo eise?* he reads. *Where the hell are you?*

• • •

There are dozens of them—airheads—packed into the tiny bar, jumping up and down to "Smells Like Teen Spirit," heads narrowly missing the low ceiling. Aki can feel the bass reaching up into his chest. The American is on the small podium taking his turn at airaoke, mouthing the words, his left hand wrapped around an imaginary neck, the other crunching down on invisible strings. A banner hangs over him with the competition's motto: "You Can't Hold a Gun If You're Holding an Air Guitar."

Through the darkness and fog, Aki scans the various faces and costumes, drinks in the air, arms around shoulders. There's Hello Kitty armor and fake mustaches, black leather outfits and sequined vests, tuxedos and face paint. It's like Greek Carnival.

Aki and Penelope stand against the bar, each holding a beer compliments of the American even though they've never liked the bitter taste of it. Penelope is looking at her phone, its screen lighting her face, her bracelets sliding down her arm. He asks her who it is but can't make out her response. He knows it must be her parents anyway, checking in on her. They think she's in Rhodes on holiday with friends.

The Viking squeezes past Aki, presses his sweaty body against him, and leans across the bar for another drink. He tousles Aki's big curls, his trademark. "Love the hair, brother," he says. Air Jesus is still on the podium, his face contorted. He sings along with the others in unison. *With the lights out, it's less dangerous, here we are now, entertain us.*

Later that night, back in the American's room, Penelope

is asleep in bed. Aki and Air Jesus stand on the balcony, arms folded, having a cigarette. Aki can see the cross atop the Oulu Cathedral. Below, the last partygoers are stumbling back to the hotel, chanting Finnish drinking songs.

"Things are pretty messed up in Greece I hear, huh?" the American says.

Aki nods, blows smoke. "Terrible. There's no work, especially for the young people. My brother is twenty-five years old and can't find a job." The thought of his brother conjures up a cocktail of feelings: guilt, fear, embarrassment. "That's why I want to win and be like you," Aki says and smirks.

Aki wants to make Dr. Pepper commercials. He wants his winning performance to have a half million YouTube views. He wants the grand prize too. A few months ago he cracked the neck of his guitar, so his band broke up. If he wins the tournament, he gets a hand-crafted Finnish electric signed by Brian May, the guitarist from Queen. Even when the American tells him he has a real job, that he's a graphic designer in Los Angeles, that no one makes a living on air guitar alone, Aki just lights another cigarette with the tip of the last one.

Aki can't sleep. He tosses and turns and then tiptoes out of the room, propping the door with a red high-top. He walks down the hallway, so quiet he can hear the buzzing of the lights. Television chatter and laughter escape from a room at the end of the hall. He thinks about his brother. He promised him he'd be there today, at the meeting, even though he knew he wouldn't. And he's supposed to be there tomorrow too, in front of the Parliament building with the rest of them. He's supposed to be there waving the Greek flag, shouting nationalist slogans, hurling rocks at riot police.

"We're going to save our country from these fucking government traitors and these illegal foreigners, you understand?" his brother had said to him once at the kitchen table, his eyes a burning sun Aki had to look away from. "We're going to bring Greece back to what it was."

People say the Golden Dawn, as they're called, are neo-Nazis. They've been accused of killing immigrants—Albanians, Pakistanis, Bulgarians. Aki's brother doesn't answer when he asks him if it's true. Aki creeps back into the room and lays down. He can't get Nirvana out of his head. *With the lights out, it's less dangerous.* He shakes Penelope, wakes her up, and she holds him until he falls asleep.

• • •

Aki and Penelope are almost late for the bicycle tour of the city. While she swipes Finnish coffee and porridge from the continental breakfast spread, he runs over to check the standings posted in the reception. He scans the board and finds his name. He's made it through. In his head, he sings, *Hey I, I, oh, oh, I'm still alive.* The airheads are waiting outside the hotel. "*Bravo, Aki mou,*" Penelope says and wraps herself around his arm. *Bravo, my Aki.* They grab hands and hurry out, Aki tearing off a bite of a rye bread roll.

"Let's go, little Greek bro with the fro," the American says, straddling the seat of a yellow single-speed cruiser with high handle bars, his backpack in the rear basket. He's holding up a tandem bike for Aki and Penelope.

Aki is ranked last among those remaining so he'll be the first to perform that night to the secret song chosen by the tournament organizers. The American is atop the leader board. He'll have the advantage of seeing everyone else perform first before he has to get on stage, so Aki will have to wow the judges from the get-go, earn triple sixes—the max score, leave no doubt.

The airheads head toward the city centre, the American leading the way with Aki and Penelope beside him, an unimposing bike gang, maybe thirty of them, a United Nations of girls and guys with crazy hair and body art.

They get to the Market Square along the waterfront, surrounded by wooden storehouses turned into restaurants and handicraft shops, bicycle tires rattling over cobblestone. Locals sit and drink coffee, and old women carry bags full of vegetables and fruit, reindeer meat, and honey. The airheads hop off their bikes to take photographs with the stout bronze Policeman statue and to buy souvenirs—bottle openers fashioned from antlers, hats made of reindeer fur. They take videos of themselves playing air accordion next to a real accordion player in a white beret.

Aki's phone vibrates in his pocket and it's another message from his brother. *Pousti*, is all it reads. *Faggot.* He imagines they're preparing for the rally now, handing out torches and flags and stacks of leaflets. When Aki stares at the message—*Pousti*—he feels anger, though he's not sure at what—at his brother, at himself, at the American who's smiling now and making the peace sign for a picture with the accordion player?

They ride on to see the Oulu Castle and then across the

river estuary toward Nallikari Beach, hidden behind a curtain of pine trees.

"So what else do you like to do, dude?" the American says. "What do you want to be when you're older?"

"I don't know," Aki says, pushing his hair from his face. "Music is the only thing I like. The only thing I'm good at."

Aki lives in a poor suburb of Athens. He's never done well in school, hates reading. He has one photo of his dad and knows just that he built boats at one time so his brother is the only real role model he's had. Penelope, on the other hand, is smart, has a good family, stays out of trouble. Aki constantly wonders what it is she likes about him. He's sure she'll leave him eventually, though she swears she never will, and move to London or Munich to become a doctor or businesswoman like so many other Greeks.

When they get to the beach, the airheads leave the bikes and run for the water. Aki and Penelope sit down amidst sunbathers, take off their high-tops and bury their olive feet in the brown sand. Aki pulls his shirt over his head, exposing his gold cross and long, bony torso. The air is cool and carries in the stench of everything that's out there, alive and dead, regenerating.

"So," Penelope asks, "are you ready?"

Aki nods. He looks at the American, his new friend and mentor, splashing through the shallow waters, chasing the Viking, and he gets excited at the thought of unseating him, taking over as the air guitar world ambassador, grabbing endorsements for everything from potato chips to shampoo. "*Sagapo*," he says to her. *I love you.*

Back at the hotel, the flat screen in the lobby is tuned in to the BBC news. It's showing the demonstration in Athens turned violent. Aki and Penelope stop to watch. "*Po po*," Penelope says and puts her hand to her lips. *My God.*

Black-clad youth holding torches and waving flags chant Anti-everything slogans. Anti-government, anti-Turkish, anti-American. Fifteen-hundred left-wing Greeks have unexpectedly descended on the demonstration to protest against the Golden Dawn. They've taken over Constitution Square. Burning tires send plumes of smoke into the sky, and Aki swears he can smell their bitterness. Riot police fire tear gas into crowds and down subway stations. Protestors hurl petrol bombs and stones. Golden Dawn chants boom through the television speakers: "Foreigners out of Greece!"

Aki looks for his brother, though he hopes he doesn't see him. He hopes he's run the hell away from there, but he knows him better than that.

"Glo-ry to Greece!" the chants continue. "Glo-ry to Greece! Glo-ry to Greece!"

• • •

Aki stands at the side of the stage. He leans forward to look out as people continue to pour into the square. Thousands of them. Photographers with giant lenses line the front row. A young girl in pigtails sits on her father's shoulders. Aki's outfit is less ornate than most, and he now worries it will count against him: black knee pads, black Megadeth T-shirt (from the *So Far, So Good…So What!* album), and zebra-patterned stretch pants. His right knee trembles. He has one minute to prepare for a song he's just heard for the first time—"Plane Crash" by The Toadies. He shakes his hair so it falls over the acne on his forehead and does his cross three times. The emcee stomps across the stage, energizing the crowd. "The axes are invisible, but the chops are real..." and there's applause before Aki hears the emcee shout his name. "From Greece, ladies and gentlemen, Air-is-totle!"

Aki trots out and pauses for a moment, center stage, locates Penelope on the left, three rows deep. He points to the sky indicating he's ready to begin. When the song kicks in—an angry, punk-rock riff followed by a high-pitched scream—Aki thinks he knows what he has to do so he races to one end of the stage and then to the other, leaps as high as he can and kicks. The hot lights flash, blue and red and gold. He bangs his overflowing head of hair because that's what he has over all the other competitors, even over the American. He doesn't know the words but tries to mouth along anyway. He hears "*Bravo*!" yelled out and it can only be Penelope, so he bangs his head some more. He gets lost hammering away at the strings of his air guitar, punching at the air to the drum beat, jump-kicking like he's bursting through a brick wall, and miscalculates sixty seconds. When the song cuts out he's on his knees, thinking about pulling a limbo-of-sorts maneuver but not quite, and he blows the ending, a gymnast who doesn't stick the landing.

When the judges go around and raise their scores—5.4, 4.9, 5.2—Aki knows his journey is done. He knows there's no chance it'll be good enough. He knows he's leaving Oulu with nothing.

He rushes off the stage and doesn't even look for Penelope.

He pushes his way through the crowd, not responding when people pat him on the back and compliment his performance. He finally breaks through to open space and then lights a cigarette, disappears into the Oulu streets, smoking one after another as the sun sets. No matter how far he walks, though, he can't escape the music. He eventually heads back to the hotel. The concierge eyes him as he cuts through the lobby and Aki glares back. He hurries up to the room and goes straight for the American's mattress. He lifts it up, heavier than he thought it would be, and manages to shove it off and wedge it between the bed frame and the wall. He does the same to the other mattress too. He grabs a red vase and shatters it against the floor, then tears the art from above the desk, a black-and-white print of Helsinki at night, and smashes it over the headboard. He stops to catch his breath, the room throbbing from the bass below. And he realizes he's a failure at even this, the greatest of rock n' roll acts, because the music is drowning out his show.

Aki steps out onto the balcony and lights a cigarette. He can see the American performing on the big screen beside the stage. He's in tight black leather pants and a leather vest, a silver-studded belt, and a neon green tie and sunglasses. The square is packed, the air thick with machine-made smoke. The American is a performer, he's Hollywood, and doesn't miss a detail. His foot is pressing an imaginary pedal as his hair whips across his face. He's singing along to the words flawlessly like he's been practicing for years. *We know what we really want, we know what we really want.* He points to the crowd, then flings the air guitar around his back, catching it in front.

Aki comes back inside and takes the American's Euros

from the nightstand. He rifles through his open suitcase spread across the floor and pulls out his wallet, iPhone, iPod, and MacBook. Outside, he can hear the crowd erupting. Cigarette ash peppers the American's folded clothes. The door opens and, for a moment, Aki hopes it's the skinny concierge so he can throw him to the ground and pound on him with his real Greek hands, real Greek fists. But it's not, it's Penelope. She doesn't say anything, just stares at him, shakes her head, gives a look of disgust. And he imagines that now, finally, the epiphany has set in that she deserves far better than him. Aki keeps taking things from the American's suitcase and stuffing them into his own backpack. Penelope walks away and he doesn't follow. "*Asto dialo*!" he shouts after her, as loud as he can. *Go to hell!* He regrets it immediately. He grabs his complimentary Air Guitar World Championships sack and the American's too and storms out of the room leaving the door wide open.

• • •

When Aki steps out of the hotel and into the crowd, he hears the emcee say, "Where's Air-istotle? Has anyone seen Air-istotle?" And then young Fins in scarves and sunglasses are howling and pushing Aki up toward the stage. The competitors are huddled together and clapping as the grand prize—a real, clear-body lucite guitar—is strapped over the American's neck.

While Aki shuffles forward, his phone vibrates. He presses it to his ear and cups his hand over his other ear. "*Mama*?" he says. He can't make out what she's saying, but can tell she's speaking quickly. Something about his brother, he thinks. She sounds panicked. The intro to "Rockin' in the Free World" rumbles out of the speakers and the emcee invites the audience members to pull out their own invisible instruments. Aki loses the call. "*Mama*? *Mama*?"

On stage, a group jam breaks out. A shirtless Electric Ninja body surfs the crowd, his blond wig flapping like flames; Van Dammage and Buenos Air-ace hold each other up with their backs and pound away at their air guitars. Aki looks out at the mass of people, cameras flashing, but Penelope is nowhere to be seen. With a bag full of clothes and electronics pushing down on his shoulders, his legs feel heavy. He's between the American and the Viking who are hopping up and down. The Viking ruffles Aki's hair and the American throws an arm over him and screams: "You'll be here again next year, brother." He hands Aki the electric guitar and hangs the strap over him. "This'll be yours one of these days."

Aki runs his calloused fingers against the raw strings. He holds the smooth neck in his hand, starts to strum with the other. He almost forgot what a real guitar felt like and now he doesn't want to let go. He keeps searching for Penelope. He begins to imagine this doesn't have to be their last time in Oulu. Confetti falls from the rafters. He plays along to the verse—E-D-C, E-D-C, E-D-C—while his phone vibrates in his pocket.

B-SIDES

by Beth Gilstrap

THE sky and the trees bellow same as anything. When I drop the needle on the record, the arm is slight enough it could dissipate like chalk dust banged loose from erasers. People can only brace themselves for so long before everything's upended. I've known my share of tough. Mama and Daddy, my grandma, and hell, even Maddie in her way, but all the effort that goes into being hard wears you down just the same. A few seconds in, the song catches. Pick it up. Move past it. Same as anything.

I wasn't supposed to touch my mother's record player when I was little. She'd tucked her albums in the bookcase like squares of gold, well protected from dust in their plastic sleeves and resting in alphabetical order. The artwork. The feel of the vinyl. The variations in sounds, some so rough-and-tumble they'd hurt my ears with their screams and guitar solos and the smashing thump of the drums. Some, like that Nina Simone record, with a sound that made my shoulders ache while I twirled on orange shag carpet. It was almost more than I could bear.

ABBA made me bouncy and when I put them on I'd practice my somersaults off the edge of the couch into a mountain of pillows. Black Sabbath made my head fuzzy. Chicago: rock with horns. The *Dirty Dancing* soundtrack was one of my favorites. I'd try to move like they did in the movie, but my hips were narrow and awkward. Some of the records were smaller with only a few songs. Forty-fives. The Temptations. But my favorite was that Nina Simone record. I would stretch my arms out into the air and above my head and I'd point my toes, trying to remember what I learned in ballet. It was all about the turnout, but I never really knew what that meant. I'd try to sing along, taking deep breaths to stretch the notes but my voice was high and thin and didn't fit Nina's frame. I sounded better with ABBA or Culture Club or even Madonna. I didn't know anything about singing then and I don't now. I still only sing when I'm alone. Tonight was no exception. I wonder sometimes about aesthetics and taste buds and if my own voice, the voice that to me sounds so much like a fiddle that hasn't been tuned, might come across as velvet to another.

Dad says I have to call my mother. Since she's sick this might be my last chance to mend what's torn. I'm supposed to let it go—the way my mother seemed flustered and distracted even when she read to me when she still lived with us. How her voice fell flat, reflecting the cotton in her head, the bubbling, festering depression. Even Curious George droned low. I like to think I can remember when Mother took painkillers, secret flashes of a hand going to her mouth and a head flung back and the countless sips of Diet Coke. I think I even remember her eyelids wavering. But the only thing I'm sure of is that right before Mother left, she had napped a lot. Curled up with her fuzzy avocado green blanket on the sofa, she looked at the television. *All My Children*, *One Life to Live*, and *General Hospital* all in a row. She'd get up and cook when she had to, but Dad eventually started picking up takeout on his way home from work. I loved the way sweet sesame chicken stuck to my teeth in a greasy crunch. Those nights Mother barely ate, but Dad and I would sit at the kitchen table and laugh about eating like bachelors. He would share his Kung Pao shrimp, and I would offer up the smallest piece of chicken I could find. He'd never take it. We'd swap fortunes. I always wished I'd gotten my father's. His always seemed better but he'd say, "Baby, I'd give anything to have yours."

I'll call her tomorrow, after breakfast, when the wine's worn off. Tonight, it's too much. Tonight, I'll finish the bottle and listen to records in a room where so much of my life has been spent. Filled with specters of who I once was and all those that have died or left, never far below the surface. All you have to do is look at the remnants of old paint colors around the baseboards. If Maddie weren't sleeping at Martin's, she'd at least get drunk with me and try to make me laugh. We could dance stupid to the Bangles or something. The dogs aren't exactly talking back to me. Lying on the floor with records spread everywhere and a bottle of wine probably isn't the best idea I ever had. Maddie would say I'm getting all Bette Davis on her, but I figure I'm entitled to mope as I see fit. I don't know what I'm supposed to feel. My mother has been trying for almost a year now to get reacquainted with me. She's supposedly sober two years. Hell, even Dad talks to her now. I can't seem to get past the nights of wishing she would call, wondering where she was, dreaming of the last pie she'd made, its buttery feel in my mouth. I've been skeptical of everyone as long as I could remember. Maybe it was her fault. Maybe it's just my nature. I don't trust anyone other than Maddie and Dad, and now he's moved away and Maddie's in a serious relationship. On top of it all, the guilt over breaking Linda's heart is stubborn and dug in. Now it's come down to just me and wine and records in this house that passed to me.

"You have to call her, baby girl," Dad said.

"I know. Just don't rush me."

"You may not have long. It's in her lymph nodes."

"What would I say to her?"

"I don't think it's the what that matters."

Drifting off, belly down on the carpet, I wonder if she's well enough to make a pie. Sometime later, I'm shot in the neck. Outside Maddie's old apartment as we walk to her car together. Maddie's clad in black skinny jeans and a red velvet tank. A hooded man walks up, shoots Maddie in the head; I fall to the asphalt and spread my hands. My hands move to the warmth at my neck. "I don't have any money, but take my cards," I whisper. Just in case, I pray, "I do believe, Dear Lord, please. Please forgive me." I don't know why I'm always praying in my dreams.

When I wake, I'm sweat and prayer stained. The arm bounces in pops of static. After dumping the last bit of wine down the kitchen sink, I go to the porch to watch another summer storm and to let the breeze dry me out. The screen door screeches behind me and I sit down on the front steps, lie back on the porch looking up at the corroded light fixture. My grandmother used to stand on a ladder and polish that brass. Once, she did it in the middle of July. She had set up a kiddie pool out front with an umbrella and a picnic blanket for Maddie and me. Maddie's grandmother lived down the street from mine and we'd both spend time there in the summers when school was out. We met the summer after kindergarten at a neighborhood barbecue at Rachel and Jack Sanders's house. We'd rolled down their steep hill—Maddie in her starched Sunday dress and me in my denim jumper. We were the only girls our age in the neighborhood so we were a natural pair, and from what our grandmothers said, we both had a rebellious streak that was like kindling. There was a picture of that day – all the neighborhood folks sitting at a picnic table with burgers and chips, the sun bouncing off bare shoulders and knees. Women wore Bermuda shorts and men wore white T's and jeans, and the moment seemed made up, everyone's hair looked so curled and gelled, their faces softened by oak shade. I don't remember eating anything that day, but I remember Maddie and my mother's rage when she saw the grass stains on my jumper. She and Dad had argued about it in the car on the way home. Dad didn't think it was a big deal, but she muttered about how we couldn't have anything nice. Anyway, she complained about me, like she always did. I was never good enough.

Maddie and I stayed outside most summer days, playing house on the front porch or playing hide-and-seek and red light, green light. Grandma made us turkey sandwiches and chips with homemade dip. That day she'd set out the pool for us, she'd decided to polish all the brass in the house and she started with that fixture on the porch; she wore red rubber gloves up to her elbows and a kerchief over her hair. "Can't contain this mess in the humidity," she'd say, patting her head. Grandpa would laugh at her, tell her she looked like a ragamuffin and he didn't know he'd married some scarf-headed woebegone. She'd tell him to take a look in the mirror at his overalls and the dirt under his nails and then they'd talk. "I don't hear you complaining about the spit shine I put to this house," she'd say. They always did their chores with softhearted teasing. Grandpa never recovered from losing her in the car accident. The house never did look right after she died, but I've got it shining now even if I don't have anyone to share it with.

Sitting up, I dig into tender elbows. Rain's coming down so hard it bounces up onto my bare feet and runs between my toes. I've never been around anyone with cancer before. I'm not sure how to react to it or even if I want to go near my mother, despite everything. Grandpa was sick for a long time, but Dad had taken care of him. Sure, I'd go visit in the hospital, but it was a distant sort of visitation meant more as support for Dad than anything. I wasn't the one making decisions about his care or talking to doctors and nurses about his stats and DNRs and all that. That was something for older people to deal with. I took Dad cheeseburgers or Chinese since he barely ever left the hospital once they moved him to hospice, but I didn't linger near Grandpa. The way his lips caked made it difficult to even look at him. His mouth had a stiff, waxy look about it already. Grandpa didn't know anyone was even in the room anyway, and when they had to resort to keeping him restrained, I stopped going upstairs altogether. I'd just meet Dad in the smoking area downstairs.

"How's he doing?" I'd ask, lighting his cigarette.

"Same," he'd say, "Hanging on but not eating. They're asking me about putting in a feeding tube."

"What do you think you'll do?"

"I reckon I'll tell them no. I don't think he'd want to live that way. And just so you know, I certainly wouldn't. Sign the Do Not Resuscitate for me."

"Please don't talk about that, Daddy," I'd begged, flattening ash segments with my boot.

"Well, this is what happens when you don't, sweetheart. We wind up not knowing what the sick person wants. It's just guesswork and it's the living that have to hold all the guilt of it. It's enough to kick my habit into high gear. Give me another light."

I wonder if Dad will come back to visit Mom, if he can deal with seeing her sick. I remember them together when I was young. That summer of the kiddie pool, they'd left me with my grandparents to take a sort of second honeymoon up in Asheville. Dad told me they'd stayed in a log cabin and hiked and whitewater rafted with two other couples. There was a photograph of Mom standing on the riverbank in jean shorts and a yellow halter, her long hair braided and hanging down to her chest. She was tan and healthy-looking. Dad was in the raft, looking triumphant with an oar over his head. Dad said the raft had tipped later that day – Mom had fallen in and come away with purple and black from hip to shin. She'd blamed Dad for making her go, and according to him, she had downed a bottle of Jack to numb the pain. He spent that evening tending a fire outside the cabin and toasting marshmallows with one of the other couples – Rod and Ruby. He recalled they were trying to have a baby. Dad never saw them again after Mom left. He guessed Mom didn't either. "They were too good for our dysfunction," he'd said. But he still talked about that week, even now, and wondered if their family stayed together.

The next morning, I wake sure of what to do. I still feel that shot to the neck. In it is a longing for my Dad and Maddie. Fire in the flesh, fading to white. Felt like losing Maddie to Martin. Losing Grandma to a city truck. Losing Dad to the sway of Myrtle Beach. Losing Celia to the wind, her fair hair flailing. And my own chucking of Linda. It was in the slow movement of warmth from inside to my grasping hand, to the asphalt, to the drying sun. I wonder if Mom has anyone besides Aunt Brenna. She's divorced for the third time, after all. I am her only child. She probably squandered any friends she had when she was still drinking. We are both good at pushing people away, from what Dad says. And hell, if Dad could still find some shred of the pie baker in her, maybe I can too. I want to believe in what Dad believes. He says I have to forgive Mom and move on before I'll ever be content or find a healthy relationship. I have my doubts. But still, there's a pang when I think about my mom hooked up to IVs and her body weakening. Isn't she, despite everything, my creator, my blood, my beginning?

This is how it will end, I think, as I knock on the door. The geraniums on Mom's steps have wilted. Buds that have dried before they bloomed stand stiff in clusters. The crepe myrtle is in full bloom, and it burns my eyes and tickles my nose. It takes Mom a while to get to the door. I wonder if she's coming and then, finally after I fiddle with the mailbox and pick at the dead blossoms, she opens the door. I'm surprised that she looks much the same as she did when she came to the store a while back. Her eyes are darker but she doesn't look sick. When she smiles, her eyes scrunch and the lines in her cheeks become more defined. She comes outside and wraps her arms around me. She collapses into a wet sob on my shoulder and I feel like pushing her off me, but I don't. I let her cry.

"I'm so glad you're here. It's almost worth being sick for you to be standing here on my porch." She leans back, wipes her eyes.

"You shouldn't say things like that, Mom. How are you?"

She cocks her head when she hears me call her Mom. "First, let's get something cool to drink. What can I get you?"

"Coke?"

"I have Diet," she says.

"How about just ice water then?"

"Be right back. I'd invite you in but the house is a mess. I haven't felt much like cleaning since I started chemo."

"I don't care about messiness."

"That's not what your father says. No, I'd be too embarrassed to let you in here."

I wait on my sick mother to serve me a cool drink in the blistering heat of late summer. Heat waves rise from the sidewalk and everything beyond looks fuzzy from the haze. It always smells like pine needles when it's this hot. I wonder how much time my mother has left in this world. Based on what Dad says, it's months maybe unless this experimental drug they're trying slows the progression. My chest tightens as I think about IVs going into Mom's arms. I can't stand needles. Last time I got a flu shot, I passed out. I'd gone with Dad to a flu shot RV they set up in the mall parking lot last winter. I felt myself slipping from consciousness into the spinning black and brightness of a faint. Dad had seen it many times before. I passed out whenever I saw any kind of real injury or whenever I gave blood. Even the medical shows on TV make me uncomfortable. There's nothing like a rerun of *ER* or *House* to give me panic attacks and disrupt my sleep. Dad laughed at the way the nurse freaked out over my convulsions. To him, it was no big deal. He told the nurse I would be fine, just to give me a minute, and the nurse yelled at us both for not telling her what to expect. "How was I to know for sure?" I asked. "I never passed out from a shot before." We joke about how when I pass out next time Dad will just step over me and leave me there on the ground twitching.

I sip from my bendy straw. The water has a squeeze of lemon and a sprig of mint. "Fancy," I say. "But good."

"Thanks," Mom says. "I'm having a problem with citrus, so I figured I'd just give it to you. I've got several lemons in there you can take home. I have sores in my throat. One of the many joys of chemotherapy."

"So how's that going?" I ask, noticing the purple-brown spots on her arms and hands. No one ever tells you how to ask questions like this. Anything you say to someone in treatment feels wrong.

"It's really kind of boring sitting in the infusion room for hours. I get annoyed with people who want to swap cancer stories, so I just pop on my headphones and close my eyes most of the time. Sometimes I fall asleep, but I usually can't because whatever chemical they're putting in my veins burns. I get cold. They cover me with warm blankets. I like that part, that and all the junk food that's left in the kitchen for us. People love to bring donuts and cookies to cancer patients. You'd think they'd bring something healthier and sometimes you see a fruit basket, but that's rare. Though I guess I would rather have a chocolate frosted donut if I'm on my way out. The nutritionist says to eat antioxidant-rich foods and all that, but I don't think eating spinach and blueberries is going to cut it. Maybe that's a bad attitude, I don't know."

"I don't know what to say."

"You don't have to say anything, baby. Just sit with me," she said. "But the worst part is the God junk. I don't know what I'm supposed to say to people when they tell me they're praying for me. Great, thanks. Thanks for that wishful thinking you're doing for me. But they're trying to be polite and supportive, so I don't want to say I don't believe anymore, that I've put any faith I've got left in the doctors."

"I imagine that does get weird. All those serenity prayers and psalms. We were never really religious. Not like Maddie's family." I fidget with my straw and my eyes water. "Your geraniums don't look so good, Ma."

"No, I guess they don't," she said.

We sit for a while staring at the street. Neighbors drive by. The chickens out back fuss at each other before settling back down again and the trees seem to stretch in the lateness of the afternoon. I hate this time of year. I long for October or November, a time when I don't have to squint every time I forget my sunglasses because all of creation's sun-bleached, even my damn eyelids. Even my arm hair has turned blonde. I run my finger down my arm and look over at Mom, sitting with her knees up in her rocker. She looks content with her hair pulled up in a scrunchie, the freckles on her face more pronounced than the last time I saw her. She had started to look like her mother, Angela. The last time I saw her was before Mom left. Angela died when I was a teenager and all I could remember about her was that she made good peach ice cream. Dad used to talk about how beautiful she was with her auburn hair and long legs. "No one had a better-looking mother than your mother," he said. "I wish you could have known her better. She was something else. Had a walk, that woman. Your Mama's got it." And as she stands and stretches, her knees crack but she walks out to the mailbox with a gait that makes me understand at long last what Dad sees. When she isn't running from everyone and throwing a chemical veil over herself, Mom has grace. Her shorts are too short for a woman her age, but she carries it well with her bare feet and white tunic. I wipe my eyes. She sees me and I look away, toward the haze.

"We should get you a porch swing."

"Now there's a plan," she says. "Come on, doll, let's go inside—as long as you don't mind the mess."

"I'll try not to."

"That's good enough for me."

I walk in behind her and she stretches out on the sofa. I grab a pillow and sit with my back to her on the floor, propped up by the sofa. The room smells like our house did when I was a girl – of butter and stale coffee. There's a document on the coffee table about Avastin, the drug that might save her. I read the whole thing and learn about organ tears and heart attacks and all the strange side effects this drug can cause. Bone pain happens in most patients. I wonder if bone pain is like when I broke my pinky toe and it sent a wave of heat up my leg and spots to my eyes and I hit the ground like a falling limb. My blood radiates. I wonder how my mother will survive this. She's never been known for emotional strength and stability, but she has a calmer air than me up there on the couch with her toes dancing as she reads the latest issue of *Entertainment Weekly*.

"It looks like Aerosmith's going to tour again after all," she says, "I hope I'm well enough to go."

"Did you know I have your record player? You didn't take it with you when you left and Dad had it all those years and when he moved, he gave it to me. It's still in that same bookcase."

"I have one I bought a while ago. But that one was a wedding gift from your father. It was all about the music for us. More than watching TV or going to the movies. When we were young, we went to every concert we could find the money for. Both of us were wannabe musicians, I guess. I could tell you stories," she said, putting her magazine down on the coffee table.

"Ah, the stories," I said, pulling a pillow down from the red sofa I'd slept on so many times when it was still in my store. I held the pillow in my lap – a shield against something I couldn't put my finger on. "Did you really see Kiss?"

"Where do you think I got the T-shirt?" she asked with

glassy eyes. "I was convinced I was going to get on the bus with them. Your dad even waited out behind the Coliseum with me. That was back when he still got a kick out of my whims." She pulled a chenille throw off the back of the sofa and over her legs. I still felt the heat coming in through the crack under the front door. "Tell you what," she said. "I'll let you have it when I'm gone."

"Gee, thanks," I said, almost breathless. "I better let you get some rest. Do you need anything before I get going?"

"I can't ask anything more, sweetheart."

When I stood, my leg was asleep. I rubbed it, feeling the limb prickle back to life. Her eyes grew heavy. I held the doorknob, waiting, failing to push past the awkwardness of wanting to embrace her and not knowing how.

In my mind, I hug her.

THURSDAY NIGHT KARAOKE

by Trevor Corkum

THURSDAY NIGHT KARAOKE

THEY arrived alone, mostly, or in ragged twos and threes, stumbling in from the late winter cold in their oversized cotton hoodies and bought-on-credit Canada Goose parkas, past the out-of-order ATM in the lonely wood-panelled foyer, and the corner where the cigarette machine used to stand; skirting the Thursday evening dart league in the fluorescent-lit adjacent lounge where somebody's bawdy grandma was drinking double shots of rye and the teary-eyed break-up dramas were unfolding loudly and unsurprisingly near the bar—slurry-worded confessions and wounded shrieks of rage, all of it competing admirably with the late-season Leafs game up on the big screen TV and the aching bluesy B chords of some long-forgotten country band piped in from hidden speakers.

Still they did not pause.

They marched on, past the counter where thick home-cut fries and *Best of the City* ninety-nine cent wings, sauced in honey-garlic, slid through a narrow window like something wanted and contraband; and where a charismatic, dreadlocked chef bobbed his head agreeably, in recognition of some secret melody, or coked up on Colombian gold, it was really too hard to decipher.

At last they stepped into the warm back room, the half-walled, cordoned-off show lounge where pyramid-shaped billiards trophies and faded yellow competition ribbons from long decades past hung without apology alongside dusty Shriners' hats, and they deposited their bones wearily into booths, or at long sticky tables without removing their coats (like dining room castaways, eyes slightly aglow), ordering discount pitchers of Moosehead, plates of all-dressed poutine, and extra large onion rings, quietly awaiting their turn.

Meanwhile, at the front of that particular section, the host—a mullet-headed, athletically-fit *fortysomething* with a ZZ-Top concert T—expertly set up the stage, unpacking a pair of giant speakers and the borrowed VocoPro amp; unloading three, four, then five quality mics from an oversized Bauer hockey bag, and multi-coloured milk crates of beer-stained playbooks below a makeshift mini-library (with the helpful phrase PLAYBOOKS stenciled above it in bold), then the partitions that served as a dais, setting everything up into a unit, a kind of ready-made studio, a pop-up make-believe stadium, where dreams of fortune and glory—for a few blurry hours—might finally come true.

"Testing," he whispered, softly, once or twice under his breath.

He conducted his work without pause, without any hint of shame or any evidence of self-consciousness.

"Beer?" a server asked, in a slightly bored voice, cocking her hip to one side, and the host, without looking up, nodded, said he'd have a pint of Keith's with a Jägerbomb on the side.

No other voice could be heard at that particular moment in time: no idle conversations under the piped-in music or the hockey game still unfolding on every last TV. Only the sound, the echo—however real or imagined—of privately rehearsed lyrics unfurling in a roomful of brains.

They waited a few minutes more and finished the greasy food and chugged back their mugs of draught and made jokes about the weather, trying to be polite. And when they could stand it no longer they studied the songbooks in a vaguely Biblical way—as if they were lost apocryphal hymnals—and they jotted down their selections on scraps of coloured paper, wrote them out with unsharpened pencils as if making lists of wishes, until the wheezy hands of the cuckoo clock arrived with an expert tick.

The host, at nine, precisely, approached one of the stand-up mics, tested it again with a few raspy hisses, and then surveyed the assorted crowd who had gathered in the room for his musical evening Eucharist.

"Ladies and gentleman, boys and girls, welcome to Thursday night karaoke!"

The mulletted man, whom they all knew as Pokey, picked up an acoustic guitar, expertly tuned in advance, and began to sing a heartbreaking song from the early catalogue of Johnny Cash. They all knew Pokey in the way you know your favourite counsellor at a 12-step recovery program, the earnestness and charisma; and they knew the Johnny Cash tune too (you could see it in how they nodded, or how they tapped their nicotine fingers on rims of invisible ashtrays) and yet they did not look at him directly, did not acknowledge in any way that the evening's show had begun, by clapping or hooting or celebrating, like groupies or devoted fans. Yet something deep inside, something marked and true and chemical at the bottom of each of their hearts, unfurled its game-day flag.

As the song whimpered to an end, the crowd came marching forward, acolyte by acolyte, to deposit their folded slips into oversized sweaty hands. The host engaged in the usual banter before introducing a blond-headed gentleman in a *Finding Nemo* T-shirt up to centre stage, upon which the young man proceeded, with remarkable gusto, to launch into a rousing number by Eminem, and you, for the first time ever, quietly found your nerve, palming a half-gnawed Bowlerama pencil to jot down your own request.

You huddled inside your hoodie, biting your bottom lip, and regarded the jagged edge of your cuticle and the indented finger where a ring used to be and the hollow curve of your wrist, which you sometimes liked held down by a man who would never love you; and you took another swig of warm Coors Lite and tried to summon up the courage to make fun of the current singer, in order to make yourself feel strong.

But all you could feel in your heart was a stab of bleak comradeship.

It was the same with the next performer. A woman named

Kathy, the announcer said, who belted out the lyrics to a ballad by Dolly Parton, ragged and off-key, shaking some invisible tambourine in her puffy, upturned hand; swaying her chunky hips, steeling her smoke-ravaged voice against the years of humiliation and the indignities of her age and the cold bloated remains of the many sweet dreams of her youth, the shipwrecks of her loves and of her sorrows. Kathy, a plump woman with too much make-up, but with a tough jib of the cheek, with a ballsy stake in life, grabbed that song by the throat and throttled it like an assassin. And so you clapped a bit for Kathy, and a little for the man after her, a big guy named Gurwinder, morbidly obese, and slow, who shuffled up to take his place and then rattled off a cheesy number from the *Lion King*, stopping halfway through the song to stare out shyly into the lights, smiling like a little girl, like a small ballerina, overcome; finally taking a dramatic bow. While the rest of the crowd, the college kids and office workers, the country boys and the housewives, the unemployed and unencumbered, pounded their filthy tables and whistled very gamely to carry him across the finish line.

And then your name, announced without any fanfare, read aloud and without warning, in a honey-hued baritone, like the soothing voice of Jesus you'd heard so many times in your dreams. You were powerless to deny it—a servant to its call. So you swallowed all your courage and sashayed up to the front, through the labyrinth of chairs and tables, around the jungle of curious eyes, the droopy half-drunk stares. You noticed out one of the windows, past a collection of Victorian photos showing women in many-skirted dresses and men with antique snowshoes, that the snow had begun to fall. It was beautiful, that evening, the snow. The flakes draped the beat-up cars, softened cracked Toyota windshields and rudely dented fenders; fluttered like lost sea monkeys under murky rays of streetlamp light and settled onto the world like something holy and pure.

And so, like the others, like all those who had come before you, you took your place on the stage.

You thought: *is this what it means, to truly be alive?*

Is this what it's supposed to feel like?

You stood behind the equipment, heart pounding, and studied the miniature screen with its scroll of magical notes, and you peered out at the faces of the disenchanted and the lonely, who, in the stink of frying food, under the glare of jittery neon, seemed charmed somehow, and sad, their lives complex and profound.

(You remembered how as a child you'd gaze into your paint-flecked mirror in a strangely similar manner, imitating a rock star's motions, imagining this sort of crowd, the buzz and hopeful light, the love and careless affection.)

And then, as the music started up, as the first long chord announced itself, as it ushered in its promise and the lyrics flashed one by one across the glorious screen, you parted your chapped lips—only ever so slightly, swallowing quick and hard—and let the lonesome bird in your half-parched throat find its own way home.

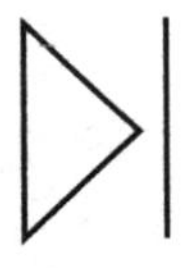

THE SONGWRITERS

SASHA CHAPIN

Sasha Chapin is a writer living in Toronto. His works has appeared in Vice, Hazlitt, and the National Post.

Twitter: @sashachapin

WENDY C. ORTIZ

Wendy C. Ortiz is the author of *Excavation: A Memoir* (Future Tense Books, 2014), *Hollywood Notebook* (Writ Large Press, 2015) and the forthcoming *Bruja* (CCM, 2016). Her work has appeared in The New York Times, McSweeney's Internet Tendency, Hazlitt, Vol. 1 Brooklyn, and The Nervous Breakdown, among other places. Wendy lives in Los Angeles.

Twitter: @WendyCOrtiz | wendyortiz.com

MENSAH DEMARY

Mensah Demary is associate web editor for Catapult. A music columnist for Electric Literature, he is also the curator and host of LIT: A Music & Reading Series. Mensah Demary lives and writes in Brooklyn, NY.

Twitter: @mensah4000 | tinyletter.com/mensahdemary

JAMES STAFFORD

James Stafford is a writer, music journalist and editor. He runs Why It Matters, a site dedicated to music and memoirs.

Twitter: @jamesostafford | wimwords.com

KHANISHA FOSTER

Khanisha Foster is a mixed race writer, performer, director, the Associate Artistic Director of 2nd Story, ensemble member of Teatro Vista, a TCGYoung Leader of Color, and has collaborated with the Citizen's Theatre in Scotland. She directed Toni Morrison's The Bluest Eye and the adaption Guess Who's Coming to Dinner. She can be seen in the film Chicago Boricua, is writing her memoir, HEROIN(E), screenplays, and is published in the anthology Briefly Knocked Unconscious By A Low Flying Duck. She is currently working on a show called Code Switching. She is getting her MFA in TV and Screenwriting from Stephens College. She hosts the podcast How I Wrote That which focuses on women who write for tv and film. www.howiwrotethat.com You can see more of her work at 2ndstory.com/people/khanisha-foster and check out her blog Black, White, and Awesome.

Twitter: @KhanishaFoster | howiwrotethat.com

TROY PALMER

Troy Palmer is the Managing Editor and Creative Director of Little Fiction | Big Truths. His stories and essays can be found online at

WhiskeyPaper, The Good Men Project, and littlefiction.com.

Twitter / Medium: @troy_palmer

MEGAN STIELSTRA

Megan Stielstra is the author of *Once I Was Cool*, and her collection *Come Here Fear* is forthcoming from Harper Perennial. Her work appears in Best American Essays, The New York Times, Guernica, The Rumpus, and elsewhere, as well as National Public Radio and Chicago's 2nd Story storytelling series. She teaches creative nonfiction at Northwestern University.

Twitter: @meganstielstra | meganstielstra.com

JAY HOSKING

Jay Hosking is the author of *Three Years With The Rat* (Hamish Hamilton / Penguin Canada 2016). He obtained his neuroscience Ph.D. at the University of British Columbia, teaching rats how to gamble and studying the neurobiological basis of choice. At the same time, he also completed a creative writing M.F.A. His short stories have appeared in The Dalhousie Review and Little Fiction, been long-listed for the CBC Canada Writes short story competition, and received an editor's special mention in the Pushcart Prize anthology. He is currently a postdoctoral fellow at Harvard University, where he researches decision-making and the human brain.

Twitter: @DocHosking | jayhosking.com

CHRISTOPHER EVANS

Christopher Evans lives in Vancouver, where he attends the University of British Columbia, and works as the Prose Editor at PRISM international magazine. His fiction, non-fiction, and poetry have appeared in The New Quarterly, Feathertale, Grain, The Canary Press, Joyland, and other publications in Canada and beyond.

Twitter: @ChrisPDEvans

LEESA CROSS-SMITH

Leesa Cross-Smith is the author of *Every Kiss A War* (Mojave River Press) and the editor of WhiskeyPaper. She had her first story (ever!) published in Storychord in 2011. Her writing can be found in The Best Small Fictions 2015 and lots of literary magazines. She lives in Kentucky and loves baseball and musicals.

Twitter: @LeesaCrossSmith | LeesaCrossSmith.com

WILL JOHNSON

Will Johnson is a writer, photographer and teacher from Nelson, BC. He is also the founder of Literary Goon, a culture blog and mentorship service. His forthcoming novel is called *This Is How You Talk To Strangers.*

Twitter: @literarygoon | literarygoon.tumblr.com

STEVE KARAS

Steve Karas is the author of *Kinda Sorta American Dream* (Tailwinds Press, 2015) and *Mesogeios* (WhiskeyPaper Press, 2016). His work has appeared in several online and print publications, including the short-fiction anthologies *Friend.Follow.Text. #storiesFromLivingOnline* (Enfield & Wizenty, 2013) *Bully* (KY Story, 2015), *Saudade* (Tortoise Books, 2016), and *Road Story* (KY Story, 2016). His story, "Catching Fire," was a finalist for The Best Small Fictions of 2015. His stories, "Kinda Sorta American Dream" and "Sculpting Sand," placed second and fourth, respectively, for Alternating Current's 2016 Luminaire Award for Best Prose. He has also written literary journal reviews for The Review Review. Steve lives in Chicago with his wife and two kids.

Twitter: @steve_karas | steve-karas.com

BETH GILSTRAP

Beth Gilstrap's fiction and essays have appeared in the Minnesota review, Literary Orphans, WhiskeyPaper, Synaesthesia Magazine, and Bull, among others. Her work has been nominated for Best of the Net, storySouth's Million Writers Award, and The Pushcart Prize. Her debut story collection, *I Am Barbarella* (Twelve Winters Press), is out now, as is her chapbook, *No Man's Wild Laura* (Hyacinth Girl Press). When she's not writing or editing, you might find her on her porch swing, with a book in one hand and a drink in the other. She lives in Charlotte with her husband and enough rescue pets to make life interesting.

Twitter: @BettySueBlue | bethgilstrap.com

TREVOR CORKUM

Trevor Corkum's fiction and non-fiction have been published widely across Canada. His work has been nominated or longlisted for a Pushcart Prize, the Journey Prize, the CBC Short Story Prize, and the CBC Creative Non-Fiction Prize. He lives in Toronto, where he runs a popular author interview series called The Chat at 49thShelf.com. His novel *The Electric Boy* is forthcoming with Doubleday Canada.

Twitter: @trevcorkum | trevorcorkum.com

AMANDA LEDUC

Amanda Leduc' is the nonfiction editor at Little Fiction | Big Truths. Her essays and stories have been published in The Rumpus, Tampa Review Online, ELLE Canada, PRISM International, Prairie Fire, and others. Her novel, *The Miracles Of Ordinary Men*, was published in 2013 by Toronto's ECW Press. She lives in Hamilton, Ontario, where she spends too much time on the Internet and is at work on her next novel. Amanda is also the Communications and Development Coordinator for The Festival of Literary Diversity.

Twitter: @AmandaLeduc | amandaleduc.com

ACKNOWLEDGEMENTS

Thank you Matt, Angela, Adam and everyone at Inkshares, and to all who helped get this book funded. Your generous support made these pages happen.

Thank you (of course) to all of the writers for trusting us with their work and to the editors who gave their permission for us to re-print certain pieces.

Very special thanks to Megan Stielstra who provided some much needed guidance and assistance early on.

Extra special thanks Michelle, who is everyting. And to Amanda and Beth, who are everything else.

Most importantly, thank you for reading.

—Troy Palmer, Little Fiction | Big Truths

littlefiction.com | @Little_Fiction

LIST OF PATRONS

This book was made possible in part by the following grand patrons, or "Die Hard" supporters, who preordered the book on Inkshares (inkshares.com) Thank you.

Audrone LeBreton

Benjamin Barnes

Christopher Palmer

Christopher Puchta

James Stafford

Leah Mol

Michelle Palmer

Matej Novak

Shawn Syms

Sierra Skye Gemma

PUBLICATION CREDITS

"Elliott Smith Is Sad, Like You" by Sasha Chapin was originally published online at Hazlitt in October 2015. (http://hazlitt.net)

Megan Stielstra's "Stop Reading and Listen" was originally published in her essay collection, *Once I Was Cool* (Curbside Splendor, 2014)

A slightly different version of Wendy C. Ortiz's "Mix Tape" originally appeared online at The Nervous Breakdown in May 2013 (http://thenervousbreakdown.com), and sections appeared in *Excavation: A Memoir* (Future Tense Books, 2014).

"Analogue" by Jay Hosking, "If They Had Music" by Will Johnson, and "Thursday Night Karaoke" by Trevor Corkum were originally published online at Little Fiction | Big Truths in March 2012, Decemeber 2012, and March 2015, respectively. (http://littlefiction.com)

A slightly different version of Leesa Cross-Smith's "My Lolita Experiment" was originally published online by Atticus Review in April 2015. http://atticusreview.org)

"Invisible Strings" by Steve Karas was originally published online at Pithead Chapel in June 2014. (http://pitheadchapel.com)

"B-Sides" by Beth Gilstrap was originally published in her story collection, *I Am Barbarella* (Twelve Winters Press, 2015)

IMAGE CREDITS

All title icons from The Noun Project (thenounproject.com), used under Creative Commons Attribution 3.0

Images created by:

Cristina Torres ("Elliott Smith Is Sad, Like You"), Matthieu Mercier ("Mix Tape"), Jasmine Jones ("God Is A DJ" and "Thursday Night Karaoke"), Ruben Vh ("Dance Outside Yourself"), Carlotta Zampini ("Me & Iggy & John"), Daouna Jeong ("Stop Reading And Listen"), Connor Shea ("Analogue"), Giuditta Valentina Gentile ("I Don't Think So"), Pantelis Gkavos ("My Lolita Experience"), Nicky Knicky ("If They Had Music"), Ben Didier ("Invisible Strings"), Matt Gipson ("B-Sides"), Mathies Janssen (nonfiction and fiction title pages), Pro Symbols (eject button), and Felix Brönnimann (cover).

INKSHARES

Inkshares is a crowdfunded book publisher. We democratize publishing by having readers select the books we publish—we edit, design, print, distribute, and market any book that meets a preorder threshold.

Interested in making a book idea come to life? Visit inkshares.com to find new book projects or to start your own.